The American Record in the Far East, 1945–1951

THE MACMILLAN COMPANY
NEW YORK · CHICAGO
DALLAS · ATLANTA · SAN FRANCISCO

MACMILLAN AND CO., LIMITED
LONDON · BOMBAY · CALCUTTA
MADRAS · MELBOURNE

**THE MACMILLAN COMPANY
OF CANADA, LIMITED**
TORONTO

THE AMERICAN RECORD

IN THE FAR EAST, 1945-1951

BY KENNETH SCOTT LATOURETTE

STERLING PROFESSOR OF MISSIONS AND ORIENTAL HISTORY

AND FELLOW OF BERKELEY COLLEGE

IN YALE UNIVERSITY

ISSUED UNDER THE AUSPICES OF THE

AMERICAN INSTITUTE OF PACIFIC RELATIONS

THE MACMILLAN COMPANY   NEW YORK   1952

First Printing

Printed in the United States of America

Preface

This book is a short record and interpretation of United States policies in the Far East since 1945. Its nature is more fully described in Chapter I.

The author had been contemplating a book of this kind, partly as a sequel to his earlier volume, *The United States Moves Across the Pacific*, but because of the pressures of various duties had about decided not to undertake it, when, quite without any suggestion from him, the American Institute of Pacific Relations asked him to write a survey of the American postwar record in the Far East. The Institute kindly offered to place its resources at his disposal; its staff, especially Mr. W. L. Holland, helped to make possible consultations with various experts, and facilitated access to published materials, including those specifically requested by the author. It circulated the first draft of the book among a number of specialists who embodied a high degree of competence in their fields, and who represented diverse points of view on the issues which are discussed in the following pages. To each and all of them the author is profoundly grateful, and even when he disagreed, he has profited immensely by their frankly expressed views. He would record his thanks especially to Professor M. S. Bates, Miss Miriam S. Farley, Mr. W. L. Holland, Professor E. O. Reischauer, Mr. L. K. Rosinger, Professor David N. Rowe, and Mr. I. M. Sacks.

The author has been left completely free to express his own opinions. Since it is the policy of the American Institute of Pacific Relations to express no opinions on public affairs, the author alone takes full responsibility for all views expressed in this volume.

Kenneth Scott Latourette

New Haven, January, 1952

Contents

I. BY WAY OF INTRODUCTION

THE SIX YEARS FOLLOWING THE COLLAPSE OF JAPAN in the summer of 1945 saw the ever deepening entanglement of the United States in the Far East.* This was especially marked in China, Japan, and Korea. It was also true of other parts of that vast area. In spite of the granting of formal independence to the Philippines, the United States preserved many ties with that country and acknowledged a responsibility for its welfare. To a degree that most Americans would not have believed possible a dozen years earlier, they and their government also became actively concerned in the affairs of Indochina, Malaya, Indonesia, Siam, and Burma. The United States was drawn increasingly into intimate relations with India and Pakistan. As a member of the United Nations it found itself the main support of that body in military action in Korea. In 1951 at least one outstanding American wished the United States to place its emphasis in foreign policy predominantly in the Far East, risking the onslaught of a new world war and ignoring if necessary its ties with Europe and its association with the United Nations.

In 1952 many Americans were badly confused. To them the Far East appeared very remote. They realized, perhaps vaguely, that they had become involved in World War II by way of the Pacific. They knew that they had borne the main burden of the occupation of defeated Japan, and that they had been excluded from China, where American power had been decisive in turning the scales against Japan. They wanted to get on with their lives, their usual occupations, and the lives of their sons and their

---

* The phrase "Far East" has never been accurately defined. In this book, for the sake of convenience, it is used to denote the area extending from Japan on the east to Pakistan on the west, and including the mainland of Asia and the adjacent islands.

1

communities, and were irritated and angered by what seemed to them irrelevant interruptions like the war in Korea. Thousands of them felt, and said, that someone must have blundered or they would not be in such a predicament.

Being human, they put the blame on those in control of their government. They criticized the President, as the head of the administration, and the Department of State, the chief organ for the conduct of foreign affairs. They were disposed to hold accountable not only the current incumbents of these posts but also those who had held them during and after World War II, for it must have been mismanagement by them, so it was widely said and believed, that had brought the nation into its present plight. Many declared that, caught in the current of day-by-day events, their government had had no policy, had been as perplexed as the average citizen, and had muddled along blindly.

Under these circumstances there is need for a brief review of these six years which will attempt to trace the course of events in their main outlines, stressing the share of Americans and especially of the government of the United States. It should point out the crucial decisions, ask what were the possible alternatives, and, on the basis of known facts, try to see what the outcome would have been had some other course been followed.

Such an account should take notice of all phases of American activity, including that of private individuals, especially business and cultural interests, but should give its main attention to the most debated side of American action, that of the government of the United States in its various branches and aspects. It should give recognition to the main currents of American public opinion and party politics in so far as these affected the Far Eastern policy of the United States. It should also note the interplay of various branches of the government, including particularly the President, the Congress, the Department of State, and the armed services.

It is of prime importance that the story be seen in its world setting. Americans must attempt to understand the situation in the Far East in its over-all aspects, as well as the situation in each country and area. They must inquire what bearing American commitments in western Europe have had upon American actions in the Far East. They must note the part played by the United Nations and the implications of United States membership in that body. Throughout the story as a continuing and dominant note is the tension between the two colossi, Russia and the United States: the one used as the tool of Communism and at the same time using Communism as its tool; and the other the leading champion of democracy as Americans, members of the British Commonwealth, and much of western Europe have understood that term.

Now is not the time for an extensive or definitive work on this subject, for it will engage scholars for generations to come. Even the material now available is too voluminous to be covered adequately by one mind without the advantage of the many specialized studies through which eventually it will be digested episode by episode. Moreover, it is highly doubtful whether the full story will ever be known. Even in diplomatic history, where there are copious records in written documents, many important negotiations take place in conversation face to face or over the telephone, and the full record is not put on paper. Nor can any author, however honestly he attempts it, attain full objectivity. His predispositions inevitably determine his choice of material and his appraisal of what is important. If he tries to pass judgment on the wisdom or morality of the actors his bias will still further shape his conclusions.

The following brief book, then, makes no pretense at finality or at complete coverage. It is not purely a condensation of available facts. Its nature is rather that of an essay. It arises from a conviction that the thoughtful and concerned public will be better able to form intelligent opinions if it can see the entire story in brief compass. This little volume is meant primarily for citizens of the United States, but it may be that others will also find it useful.

The author owes it to those who may look into these pages to state at the very outset his bias so far as he is aware of it. He is an American who has confidence in the essential soundness of his native land. Being human, Americans have made mistakes, and will make them in the future. Those who have acted for the government of the United States have from time to time been guilty of errors, some of them grievous. But the author is a firm believer in the American type of democracy. He is convinced that the majority of Americans wish to do what is best not only for themselves but also for the rest of mankind, and that through the democratic process, as conceived in theory and to a not inconsiderable degree realized in practice, Americans can work their way through the problems which confront them to a clear decision. Seldom if ever is the solution perfect. At times it may seem disastrous. Yet, better than any other system thus far known to man, democracy as the greatest of Americans have understood it makes for the welfare of mankind.

The author is frankly a Christian. The standards by which he judges what is good and what constitutes the welfare of individuals and mankind as a whole are, so far as he is aware, of Christian origin. He recognizes that in its actions the United States falls far below Christian ideals, but he believes that much in American democracy derives from Christian roots. The author is, moreover, a historian by training and long practice, and he attempts to view current events in perspective as part of the age-long human drama. The author is intensely critical of Communism, which he regards as a tragic distortion of man's noblest aspirations and an enemy to those aspirations, all the more dangerous because its leading exponents are fanatically convinced that it embodies the highest destinies of man.

In spite of convictions which shape his narrative and his conclusions, the author would not make these pages a defense of the United States, American democracy, and the Christian faith, or a diatribe against Communism. Being a historian, he desires to view events as dispassionately as possible.

The author would be the last to lay claim to infallibility. For a generation, as teacher and writer, he has been specializing in the history of the Far East. As a former resident, a traveler in one or another of the portions of the world with which these pages deal, and one who counts among his most cherished friends citizens of all the major and most of the minor lands of that region, he has followed with absorbed interest the events of which he is writing. Yet he has lived so long with experts in various branches of knowledge that he is painfully aware of how mistaken they, and he, often are, even in the areas in which they are supposed to have special competence. He therefore would not presume to be oracular.

The method of treatment may require a word of explanation. First comes a chapter surveying the manner in which the United States became involved in the Far East and the main features of American Far Eastern policy and action before August, 1945. This is of prime importance, for the events after Japan's surrender arose from a long series of antecedent steps and are quite incomprehensible without an awareness of the past. Then follows a chapter describing the setting in which the United States operated. This deals both with the Far East and with the world at large, for it must be obvious to any thoughtful observer that Americans must take cognizance of the progress of events in the "one world" of which the Far East was a part, and by which it was influenced. We shall then embark on a country-by-country survey, beginning with India and moving on through southeast Asia to China and Japan, and ending with Korea. Although the United States was operating simultaneously in many countries, and although an over-all pattern can be discerned in American policy, that policy was adapted to the conditions peculiar to each country.

The order in which the countries are treated is somewhat arbitrary; but there seems to be good reason for having the story culminate in Korea, for it was there that much of American thought and action was focused in the year and a half following June, 1950. China and Japan should be treated before Korea but in close proximity to it, as the Korean crisis raised issues involving all three countries. The major part of our space must be given to these three lands, for in them the United States was most deeply involved, and to them it devoted most of its effort. A concluding chapter attempts to tie together the entire story and to formulate some inclusive generalizations.

As we have hinted, the main emphasis is on the policies of the United States government. That is largely because in the six years from 1945 to 1951 it was through their government that Americans chiefly acted. However, we must remember that the contacts of the United States with the Far East were not merely through government and its representatives. They were also made through what we call private channels—through movies, travelers, and especially merchants, bankers, students returned from the United States, and missionaries. Here was the impact of a whole people and its culture upon another vast segment of mankind.

Moreover, this process was part of a larger one—the impact of the entire Western world upon the Orient. The Occident was also represented by western Europe, in later years a waning influence so far as its governments were concerned. Yet one force which originated in western Europe, Communism, was rapidly mounting in its effect and was the major rival to the Western tradition shared by the United States. It came by way of Russia, a land which it captured following World War I after a collapse of an old order not unlike the disintegration of earlier civilizations which had been taking place in most of the Far East in recent years. It became closely associated with Russia and made its way under Russian guise and partly under Russian direction and as a Russian tool. Yet it was by no means entirely identical with Russia. It was appropriated by important elements in the peoples of the Far East, which sought the kind of dominance that the Communist Party possessed in Russia. When this book was being written they were in control of China and North Korea. Here was a movement closely associated with Russia but much larger than Russia.

This little book is not intended for those who are expert on the Far East. Many experts will dissent, some of them vigorously, from several of the interpretations which are presented here. It is rather designed for the somewhat hypothetical "general reader," the intelligent average American who wishes to have in the simplest and briefest possible form a comprehensive summary of the actions of his fellow citizens and especially of his government in Asia during these crucial years. It may also be of value to those, not Americans, who will welcome a guide through what seems to them the confused and enigmatic maze of American action in the Far East in the years after V-J Day.

These pages were written while the events which they record were recent or still in progress. Nevertheless such a record and analysis may have some value beyond the fleeting moment. At least it serves as an account of the thinking of one American in the summer and autumn of 1951. The main narrative ends with the signing of the peace treaty with Japan in September, 1951, although some later material is included. The peace treaty marked the end of a significant stage in the relations of the United States with one of the principal countries of Asia, and had widespread repercussions throughout the entire area. Yet our story ends with a comma or at best a semicolon, not a period, for American relations with Asia continued without interruption.

II. THE LONG BACKGROUND

OF AMERICAN INVOLVEMENT

IT IS IMPORTANT THAT WE RECOGNIZE AT THE OUT-
set that the six years covered in this essay were not lived in isolation from the past. The deep involvement of the United States in
the Far East after World War II was the outgrowth of a movement which had been in progress since the dawn of American
history, and the result of policies formulated at least as far back
as the closing years of the nineteenth century and the opening
years of the twentieth century. While not always pushed with
the same degree of vigor, those policies were pursued fairly consistently across the decades until they brought the United States
into the unenviable position in which it found itself in August,
1945.

It must also be recognized that the United States could not
quickly solve the problems with which it was confronted in the
Far East. Nor could it extricate itself from the Far East without
completely denying much of the course of its history. If one views
the involvement of the United States in the Far East as a colossal
mistake, as did many Americans, especially in the troubled years
which followed August, 1945, what occurred was in the nature
of a Greek tragedy. Steps taken many years earlier and in ignorance of a future which no one could have been wise enough to
forecast led to complications fraught with incalculable suffering
for Americans and their transpacific neighbors. Even if, in 1950 or
1951, the United States had attempted the impossible and had
sought to escape from the past and to withdraw completely from
the Far East, it would not thereby have solved the problem and
ended the tragedy. For here was no Gordian knot to be cut by

8

one bold stroke. For better or for worse, and much of the time it seemed for the worse, Americans had become inextricably enmeshed in a complicated web. Whatever they did affected the well-being not only of themselves and the peoples of the Far East but also, to a greater or less extent, of all the rest of mankind.

There were no easy, perfect, or quickly achieved solutions. That was partly because of the nature of the problem and partly because of the reluctance or the inability of the United States to take measures adequately to deal with them. The teeming and rapidly growing populations, the poverty of the masses, the difficult transition from a colonial status to self-rule, the reshaping of ancient cultures, and the threat and advance of Communism— these and other conditions made early or perfect solutions impossible. Throughout its course the contemporary generation would wrestle with the issues. The most that it could hope for was such a measure of wisdom that the degree of tragedy would be lightened, and that succeeding generations would find the problems less difficult and the road less arduous. With their impatience and their demand for prompt and decisive results, Americans again and again felt frustrated and were tempted to withdraw completely or to seek the way out in the application of armed force—a procedure which generally would aggravate rather than ease the situation.

The involvement of the United States in the Far East grew out of the westward drive of the American people. That drive began with the days of the first settlement of the white man on the eastern shores of what later became the United States. These settlements, whether at Jamestown, Plymouth, or elsewhere, were in themselves a westward migration from Europe. By the time that the thirteen colonies had broken with the British Empire and constituted themselves the United States, hardy pioneers had crossed the Appalachians and had begun the settlement of the valley of the Mississippi. The first western boundary of the

United States was the Mississippi River. In 1803, only twenty years after the formal recognition of the independence of the United States, the Louisiana Purchase carried the western boundary of the United States to the Rocky Mountains and perhaps farther. Even before that date the discovery of the mouth of the Columbia River by a ship from Boston had given the beginning of a claim to Oregon. In 1818, only fifteen years after the Louisiana Purchase, Great Britain and the United States signed a treaty of joint occupancy of the vast Oregon country. In 1846 the termination of joint occupancy accorded the United States sole title to the better part of that region and brought its western boundary indisputably to the Pacific. Two years later, in 1848, the treaty which ended its Mexican War gave the United States the even longer Pacific frontage of California.

In 1853, five years after the legal acquisition of California, Commodore Perry took the lead in opening Japan, for nearly two and a half centuries all but hermetically sealed against the outside world. Less than fifteen years thereafter, in 1867, Seward's purchase of Alaska from a willing Russia brought the American frontier almost in sight of Asia across the narrow Bering Strait. In 1878 the United States stepped into the mid-Pacific through the purchase of a coaling station at Pago Pago, in the Samoan Islands. The pace was quickening. Twenty years later, in 1898, the United States annexed Hawaii at the "crossroads of the Pacific." That same year, stepping across the Pacific, and not without intense debate over the wisdom of the act, the United States occupied the Philippines. A year later, in 1899, came the first of the notes formulating what became known as the Open Door policy, through which the United States expressed its interest in China.

Parallel with the westward expansion of American territory and the assumption of responsibilities in the Far East by the government of the United States went a growth in the interest

and activity of American citizens in the Orient. In 1784, the year
after Great Britain acquiesced in the independence of the United
States, the first American ship, named fittingly *Empress of China*,
sailed for Canton. In succeeding years American commerce in the
Pacific grew and became important for many a shipping family
on the Eastern seaboard. President Franklin D. Roosevelt, under
whose administration Pearl Harbor flung the United States into
war in the Pacific, inherited a lively interest in shipping and in the
Far East from his Delano ancestors, who had been engaged in the
China trade.

The China market long had a powerful fascination for Americans. Because of its huge population and the industry of its inhabitants, Americans viewed China as the largest undeveloped
market in the world. It is a familiar but no less significant fact that
among all the Western powers it was the United States that took
the successful initiative of inducing Japan to unbar her doors.
The United States had a less spectacular but highly important
role in persuading Korea to take a similar step. At least two of the
major transcontinental railroads, the Northern Pacific and the
Great Northern, felt the lure of the Far East. The first had the
Chinese yin-yang symbol as its official emblem. James J. Hill, the
creator of the other, hoped that the revenues from trade with the
Far East would swell the income of his road. Christian missionaries from the United States went to China, Japan, Korea, the
Philippines, Malaya, Siam, Burma, and India. Both American
business and American missions became important to Far Eastern
peoples.

While Far Eastern trade constituted only a small fraction of
the total foreign commerce of the United States, it loomed large
in the total scene for China, Japan, the Philippines, and Malaya.
For a time in the 1930's China Proper (excluding Manchuria) had
more trade with the United States than with any other country.
There were many years before the great depression of the 1930's

11

when the United States, because of its demand for raw silk, was Japan's best customer. The favored position of the United States in the Philippine Islands and the fact that they were within its tariff wall made the American tie primary in their economic life. American demand for the two chief exports of Malaya, tin and rubber, made American trade a major factor in its economy.

Christian missions from the United States were prominent in eastern Asia, and many Americans received their most intimate contact with that area through the missionary movement. Americans constituted the overwhelming majority in the Protestant missionary forces in Japan, Korea, the Philippines, Siam, and Burma. In China they outstripped those of any other nation, and in India they were approximately as numerous as those from the British Isles. Especially through their schools and hospitals, missionaries from the United States had an outstanding share in introducing to the largest Far Eastern land, China, the education, science, and medicine of the Occident. The Far East (including southeast Asia and India) absorbed more American Protestant missionaries than any other section of the globe. The education carried on through the Protestant churches of the United States to acquaint the supporting constituency with what was being done gave to millions information, usually sympathetic, about the peoples, cultures, and problems of eastern and southern Asia.

American Catholics were slower than American Protestants in undertaking missions in the Far East. Catholic missionaries in Asia and elsewhere came chiefly from Europe. However, after World War I the Catholics of the United States became increasingly missionary-minded. Until World War II, when Latin America supplanted it, the Far East, especially China, attracted more American Catholic missionaries than any other area.

Both factors, the hunger for markets and for opportunities to invest capital profitably, and the unselfish desire for the welfare of the peoples of the Far East partly expressed through Christian

12

missions, entered into the shaping of the Far Eastern policy of the United States. Until the acquisition of the Philippines, the United States sought no territory in the Far East. The urgent suggestion of one of the early American ministers to China that Formosa be occupied was emphatically rejected in Washington. The American conscience was always uneasy over the Philippines, and, as we are to see a little later, a combination of pressures from special business and farm interests which feared Filipino competition and from those who insisted that the United States should not hold any people in a colonial status was responsible for the action of the Congress which gave that country its independence.

Both motives entered into the Open Door policy. That policy centered on China, for the internal weakness and the potential riches of that country and its commerce tempted foreign powers to seek to partition or control it. The threat arose first from the European states, then from Japan, and later (in new ways) from Russia. The government of the United States wished to keep the door open in China to American trade and investments. Under treaties which promised it equal treatment with the most favored nation it had legal ground for objecting to special privileges granted to citizens of another state in any part of China. As early as 1900 it therefore declared its purpose to "preserve Chinese territorial and administrative entity," and in 1922 it was chiefly responsible for having written into the Nine Power Treaty the promise of the signatories "to respect the sovereignty, the independence, and the territorial and administrative integrity of China." Only thus could Americans be assured economic opportunity in China on a par with the members of other nations. However, there was also the idealistic motive, to accord to the Chinese the fullest opportunity of living their lives in their own way, with a government and institutions of their own choosing. It is significant that it was not American businessmen that pressed for the

Open Door. It was rather officials of the government of the United States, usually Secretaries of State and members of the diplomatic service, that took the initiative in formulating the policy and seeking its implementation.

Although the story is familiar to all who have followed events in the Far East over the course of the years, we do well to remind ourselves of the major steps by which, largely through the effort to obtain the observance of the Open Door in China by all the nations, the United States became ever more deeply involved. It was through them that the United States came into the position in which it found itself in 1945.

In 1899 John Hay, then Secretary of State, formally inaugurated what came to be known as the Open Door policy. The occasion was the combination of the threatened partition of China and the appearance of the United States in the Far East as a territorial power. The weakness of China had recently been disclosed through the defeat administered by Japan in the war of 1894–1895. France, Germany, Russia, and Great Britain quickly followed by acquiring leaseholds, railroad and mining concessions, and spheres of interest in China which seemed to foreshadow the partition of the country. The United States had no desire to share in the prospective division; but it had recently come into possession of the Philippines and Hawaii and had a lively concern in what was happening. If China were to be carved up among the powers, American commerce in the Empire, although more potential than actual, would suffer, for each European government would give special preference to its citizens in such portions as it possessed. Hay therefore came forward with the seemingly modest request that the governments of Great Britain, Germany, Russia, France, and Italy give assurance that in their respective leased territories and spheres of interest they would not seek special privileges for their citizens in the form of preferential tariffs or harbor dues or railroad freight rates, that they would permit the Chinese customs service to function in the collection of tariffs, and that there would be no interference with existing treaty ports and vested interests. Reasonable though these requests were in light of China's existing treaty commitments, other powers met them only with evasive responses or partial and conditional acceptance. If granted, they might entail sacrifices.

In 1900 came the Boxer outbreak, in which elements in North China, resenting foreign aggression, rose in an attempt to throw aliens out of the country. The United States, along with other powers, sent forces to rescue and protect its citizens. There was grave danger that land-hungry powers would take the occasion for further encroachments on China. To forestall this action, John Hay, still Secretary of State, sent out a circular note in which he declared it to be the policy of his government to protect American lives, property, and other legitimate interests, and "to seek a solution which may bring about permanent safety and peace to China, preserve Chinese territorial and administrative entity, protect all rights guaranteed to friendly powers by treaty and international law, and safeguard for the world the principles of equal and impartial trade with all parts of the Chinese Empire."

Here again was an attempt to safeguard American economic rights, actual or potential. Here for the first time appeared expressly the purpose of the United States to "preserve Chinese territorial and administrative entity." While this was necessary if equal opportunities with the nationals of other countries were to be conserved for American citizens, the implications were far-reaching and were to enmesh the United States ever more deeply in the Far East and to bring it into World War II. Moreover, after 1900 the United States stationed troops in Peking and Tientsin to protect its legation. They remained there uninterruptedly for nearly four decades. Nowhere else in the world have American troops been stationed so long on foreign soil, and the episode foreshadowed still further commitments of the United States in China.

Following the Boxer imbroglio the United States became especially involved in Manchuria. Russia had long cast covetous eyes upon that portion of the Chinese Empire. As early as the seventeenth century she had engaged in a minor war on its frontiers and been worsted by the Manchus, then masters of China. In the 1850's she had demanded and received from China, helpless before a British-French invasion, a huge slice of territory contiguous with Manchuria on the north and east. Before the Boxer Rebellion she had acquired in Manchuria a lease on the natural harbor fortress, Port Arthur, and the chief port, Dalny (also known as Talienwan and Dairen), and privileges of railway building under the euphemism of joint control with the Chinese. Manchuria was rich in natural resources and at that time was comparatively empty of population. Ostensibly to protect her subjects and holdings, Russia poured troops into Manchuria during the Boxer year. When the outbreak had been suppressed, she showed no inclination to withdraw them. Secretary Hay was inclined to acquiesce, for he felt the United States would not go to war to save the area for China. However, Theodore Roosevelt, then President, who had been an advocate of the seizure of the Philippines, wished a less passive policy. He sought to bring about the withdrawal of Russia from the advanced positions which she had taken in Manchuria in connection with the Boxer affair. Once again, legal justification was found in the principle of the Open Door and equal opportunity and the protection of potential or actual American trade and investment in the area.

During the war of 1904–1905 between Russia and Japan, which broke out primarily over Korea, Theodore Roosevelt was unwilling to intervene on behalf of Korea, which he felt to be a helpless pawn; but he wished to see Manchuria preserved for China. Throughout the struggle the sympathies of the American people were decidedly with Japan. Nevertheless, as the war progressed, Roosevelt began to feel that Japan might become a menace to American interests in the Far East. He acted as mediator between the belligerents, and the peace conference between them was held on American soil, at Portsmouth, New Hampshire.

From the time of her victory over Russia, tension between Japan and the United States began and, with only slight pauses, mounted, although at irregular intervals. Some of the Japanese public blamed the United States, though on quite inadequate grounds, for the fact that the peace treaty with Russia was not more favorable to Japan. It soon became clear that Japan aimed not only to control and then annex Korea but also to consolidate the holdings in South Manchuria which had been transferred to her by Russia as part of the fruits of victory. Her policies in that area seemed to threaten the Open Door. Japanese immigration to the Pacific coast of the United States was another source of irritation in both countries.

Attempts were made to ease the tension through the Taft-Katsura agreement (1905), in which Japan stated that she had no territorial ambitions against the Philippines and the United States consented to Japanese suzerainty in Korea, and through the Root-Takahira agreement (1908), in which both governments promised to support the independence and integrity of China and the principle of equal opportunity, and to respect each other's territorial possessions. However, American efforts to implement the Open Door in Manchuria made both Russians and Japanese nervous. In 1905 the American railroad magnate, E. H. Harriman, entered into negotiations with the Japanese for joint control of the South Manchuria Railway, and in 1909 he made tentative offers for the purchase of the Russian interest in the Chinese Eastern Railway, in northern Manchuria. Both projects came to naught, but in an atmosphere surcharged with suspicion they aroused fears of American designs. Partly under the prodding of the young, am-

bitious, and charming Willard Straight, American consul general
in Mukden and later head of the Division of Far Eastern Affairs
in the Department of State, suggestions were put forward that
American capital be induced to enter China and especially Manchuria to checkmate Japan. This was known as "dollar diplomacy." Secretary of State Knox made it more of an actuality. He
proposed (1909) that the six great powers, Great Britain, Russia,
Germany, France, Japan, and the United States, advance the
money to China to enable her to buy out the Japanese and Russian interests in the Manchurian railways and then have the lines
operated under an international board. The suggestion was not
welcomed and served only to draw Japan and Russia together.

However, "dollar diplomacy" was so far implemented that,
under pressure from the Department of State, American bankers
were admitted into a financial consortium of British, French, and
German interests for the building of railroads in Central China,
a consortium into which Japan and Russia soon forced their way.
President Wilson, believing that the project jeopardized the administrative independence of China, withdrew the support of
the government of the United States, and the American bankers,
who had participated in the enterprise only on the initiative of
the Department of State, pulled out.

During World War I the United States was the major check
on the measures by which Japan, taking advantage of the pre-
occupation of the European powers, sought to extend her control
over China. American diplomacy played a substantial part in
persuading Japan to modify her famous Twenty-one Demands
(1915), which, if granted in full, would have made China a
Japanese puppet. In strict consistency with earlier American
policy, Secretary of State Bryan warned both Peking and Tokyo
that the United States would not "recognize any agreement or
undertaking which has been entered into or which may be entered
into between the Governments of Japan and China, impairing

18

the treaty rights of the United States and its citizens in China, the political or territorial integrity of the Republic of China, or the international policy relative to China commonly known as the open door policy." After the United States entered World War I on the same side as Japan, the Lansing-Ishii agreement was signed in an effort at some kind of accord. In that document both powers declared that they did not intend "to infringe in any way the independence or territorial integrity of China," and that they held to "the principle of the so-called 'open door' or equal opportunity for commerce and industry in China"; but the United States recognized Japan's "special interests in China," without defining expressly what was meant.

However, when the shooting had ceased, latent friction again flared up over the disposition of the spoils of war. The United States reenforced the objection of the Chinese to allowing the Japanese to retain the former German holdings in the province of Shantung and obtained from the Japanese the assurance that the territorial holdings would be handed back and only the economic privileges be retained. While President Wilson was unable to prevent the Japanese from being awarded possession of the former German islands north of the equator, he estopped outright cession and obtained the recognition of the mandate principle for them. Moreover, feelings rose high over the allocation of the now nearly forgotten island of Yap.

The Japanese were unhappy over other actions of the United States which almost immediately followed World War I. In the disorder in Siberia which succeeded the collapse of the Czarist regime and the early stages of the revolution, the United States took the lead in preventing the Japanese from permanently moving into the area east of Lake Baikal and into the Russian sphere in northern Manchuria. The two countries also entered into what amounted to a competitive race in naval armaments.

The Washington Conference of 1921–1922 and the treaties and

conventions which came out of it eased the tension for a while. It was significant, however, that, while Japan's return of the debated Shantung properties was ostensibly on her independent initiative, the step was plainly taken to satisfy the United States. Moreover, the United States was chiefly responsible for the clause in the Nine Power Treaty (1922), already mentioned, by which the signatories, including the United States and Japan, agreed: "(1) To respect the sovereignty, the independence, and the territorial and administrative integrity of China; (2) To provide the fullest and most unembarrassed opportunity to China to develop and maintain for herself an effective and stable government; (3) To use their influence for the purpose of effectually establishing and maintaining the principle of equal opportunity for the commerce and industry of all nations throughout the territory of China; (4) To refrain from taking advantage of conditions in China in order to seek special rights or privileges which would abridge the rights of subjects or citizens of friendly States, and from countenancing action inimical to the security of such States." The United States did not undertake to guarantee these rights to China against the actions of other powers; but many Chinese later held that it had done so, and the government of the United States, while not formally admitting the obligation, acted at times as though it had made such a promise. In view of later developments, we may note that the U.S.S.R. was not a signatory of the Nine Power Treaty, as it had not been invited to the Washington Conference.

In 1924 Japanese sensibilities were deeply wounded when the United States Congress passed a law prohibiting the immigration of "aliens ineligible to citizenship"—a euphemistic phrase which was directed chiefly against the Japanese. This in effect abrogated by unilateral action the Gentlemen's Agreement under which, to allay feelings in the United States, Japan had voluntarily kept her people from coming to this country in large numbers.

The American Record in the Far East, 1945–1951

The next major crisis over the Far East, one which led, step by step, to the further commitment of the United States in that area, arose out of what was known as the Mukden incident, on September 18–19, 1931. Some of Japan's military leaders were convinced that the solution of the economic problems which confronted the country lay in the extension of Japanese rule in Manchuria and the development of its resources for the benefit of Japan. Apparently they counted on having a free hand because the United States and Europe were absorbed in the economic difficulties attendant on the depression which had begun in the United States in 1929. On a flimsy pretext Mukden was seized, and military operations were pursued which within a few months brought Manchuria and eastern Inner Mongolia under Japanese control through the transparent device of setting up the state of Manchukuo under Japanese auspices.

To deal with this palpable violation of the territory of China the existing peace machinery of the world was invoked, but proved powerless. Almost immediately China appealed to the League of Nations, citing its rights under the Covenant of that body. The League hesitantly put its machinery in motion and sent out a commission, which after about a year made its report. A few months later the Assembly of the League adopted the report, said that the League members would not recognize Manchukuo, called upon Japan to cease her military pressure on China, and ordered negotiations under the supervision of the Assembly. Japan thereupon in effect snapped her fingers at the world and withdrew from the League.

Although not a member of the League of Nations, the United States went far toward acting with the League and even sought to spur it on. In January, 1932, in conscious continuation of what by this time was its historic policy, the Secretary of State formulated in notes to China and Japan what became known, from his name, as the Stimson Doctrine. He declared that the United States

21

"can not admit the legality of any situation *de facto,* nor does it intend to recognize any treaty or agreement entered into between those Governments, or agents thereof, which may impair the treaty rights of the United States or its citizens in China, including those which relate to the sovereignty, the independence, or the territorial and administrative integrity of the Republic of China, or to the international policy relative to China, commonly known as the open door policy; and that it does not intend to recognize any situation, treaty, or agreement which may be brought about by means contrary to the covenants and obligations of the Pact of Paris of August 27, 1928, to which treaty both China and Japan, as well as the United States, are parties."

The League was not in a position to undertake sanctions other than the moral disapproval of its members. Nor was the United States prepared to do more than join in that disapproval. The effect was to stiffen Japanese resistance and to confirm the extremists in their determination to move farther into China. The episode really sounded the death knell of both the League of Nations and the Pact of Paris. American officials were to remember this history when in June, 1950, the North Koreans suddenly moved into South Korea.

For a few years an uneasy quiet seemed to settle over the relations between the United States and the Far East. Americans and their government were too deeply absorbed in working their way out of the great depression to pay more than passing attention to affairs in Asia. Japan was consolidating her position in Manchuria and eastern Inner Mongolia and slowly moving south of the Great Wall. But after December 31, 1936, when Japan (as was her legal right) denounced the treaties limiting naval armaments, both the United States and Japan began to enlarge their fleets.

In July, 1937, Japan's unremitting efforts to extend her domination over China produced a second "incident," in North China, which precipitated full-scale war between China and Japan. The

Chinese government, led by Chiang Kai-shek and the Kuomintang, or Nationalist Party, did not surrender, but was forced to
retreat westward, eventually fixing its capital at Chungking, while
the Japanese set up a puppet regime at Nanking under Wang
Ching-wei. Meanwhile the Chinese Communists had set up a government at Yenan in the northwest. The Nationalists and the
Communists, who had been virtually at war since 1927, had
reached an agreement for common resistance to Japan early in
1937; but especially after 1940 relations between Chungking and
Yenan were those of an uneasy armed truce.

Toward the Japanese aggression in China the attitude of Americans and their government was uniformly critical. The government of the United States was careful, however, to keep within
its rights under existing treaties and international law and to
move no more rapidly than public opinion would approve. In
October, 1937, President Franklin D. Roosevelt came out against
"those violations of treaties and those ignorings of humane in-
stincts which today are creating a state of international anarchy
and instability." On the same day Secretary of State Hull said
that he believed the actions of Japan in China were contrary to
the Nine Power Treaty and the Pact of Paris. Repeatedly the
United States called the attention of Japan to violations of the
rights of Americans in China. Between 1937 and the passage of
the Lend-Lease Act in 1941 the United States granted credits to
China totaling $170,000,000.

After September, 1939, when war broke out in Europe, Japan
stepped up her operations in China and began to express an interest in the Netherlands Indies. In 1940 the Japanese moved into
Indochina. In each instance the United States gave out what was
in effect a caveat. In 1940 and 1941 the United States took suc-
cessive steps to restrict exports of war materials to Japan; and in
July, 1941, together with Great Britain and the Netherlands, it

froze Japanese credits, thereby virtually suspending trade with Japan.

Negotiations to settle the outstanding issues broke down, and Japan suddenly struck at Pearl Harbor on the memorable December 7, 1941. By that deed Japan brought the United States into the war in such a way that American public opinion, which had been divided on the issue of entering the conflict, and which would have remained divided had Japan confined herself to the Far East, was instantly united against her. In attacking Pearl Harbor she lost the war, although more than three years were required to prove it to her.

From this history, so rapidly summarized, three generalizations emerge. Each of them is of the highest importance. The first is that the Far Eastern policy of the United States was in fact if not in theory bipartisan. The Open Door policy, which was its core, was enunciated and developed under Republican administrations, and was supported quite as vigorously, eventually even more so, by Democratic administrations. Democrats and Republicans differed as to what should be done in the Philippines, but no basic disagreement existed over the Open Door. That policy had become almost as much an element in the thinking of Americans in their foreign relations as the Monroe Doctrine.

In the second place, step by step the geographic scope of American action in the Far East had been broadened. At the close of World War I it was made to include eastern Siberia. During World War II, even before Pearl Harbor, the United States expressed vital interest in Indonesia and Indochina and made it clear that Japan would risk war with America if she moved into British Malaya or the Netherlands Indies.

Third, the United States had intervened more consistently in the Far East than in Europe. True, it had never kept out of a general war in Europe. Despite strenuous efforts to keep aloof, it had eventually been drawn into the war arising out of the

French Revolution and Napoleon, and into World War I. Yet, when once the fighting was over, it had withdrawn almost completely from Europe. By tradition Americans had regarded Europe as the Old World from which they or their ancestors had fled, and they had tried hard to avoid entanglement in its politics.

In contrast, American forces were continuously in the Far East from 1898 on. Even after World War II the United States had no territory in Europe; but, except for the period of the Japanese occupation, it had held the Philippines from 1898 to 1946—from 1935 on as an autonomous commonwealth. It was by way of the Pacific that the United States was drawn into World War II. Americans bore a larger proportion of the burden of defeating the enemy in the Pacific than in Europe. As the dominant power in the occupation of Japan the United States assumed responsibility for a larger population there than it did in Europe. Moreover, in the Korean war which broke out in 1950 the United States was drawn into a major campaign as it had not been in postwar Europe.

The story of American participation in the Pacific and Far Eastern phases of World War II is too complex to be summarized here; nor need it be. We shall need to return to it as we wend our way country by country through the postwar years. Here we must simply take the time to note that, while priority was given to the European phases of the struggle, the area covered by American operations in the Pacific and the Far East was very much greater than in Europe; the physical problems to be solved, such as reaching a victorious Japan across the vast expanse of the Pacific, bolstering the Chinese by the air lift from India, and re-establishing land communications with China by way of Assam and Burma, were in some ways even more formidable than those in Europe; and much less aid came from those associated with the United States in the war. Moreover, because of factors which we are to note in the succeeding chapters, the responsibilities of the United States in the Far East after World War II proved heavier and the problems even more complex and more difficult than across the Atlantic. It is to the factors, old and new, which faced the United States in the years after the defeat of Japan that we must now turn.

Selected Bibliography

A. Whitney Griswold, *The Far Eastern Policy of the United States* (New York: Harcourt, Brace & Co., 1938). The best study of the period from 1898 to 1938.

K. S. Latourette, *The United States Moves Across the Pacific* (New York: Harper & Brothers, 1946). A brief survey and analysis from the beginning of American contacts to 1946.

Herbert Feis, *The Road to Pearl Harbor* (Princeton University Press, 1950). The story of Japanese-American negotiations and of American policy from July, 1937, to December 7, 1941.

III. THE COMPLEX FACTORS, OLD
AND NEW, WHICH CONFRONTED
THE UNITED STATES AFTER
THE DEFEAT OF JAPAN

WHEN, ON THAT MEMORABLE AUGUST 14, 1945, THE news was flashed across the world that Japan had offered to surrender, the Far East entered into a new era. In postwar Asia major factors, both old and new, were at work. Because of the increasing part which it had been playing in the Far East and because of the leading share which it had had in the defeat of Japan, these factors became problems for the United States as well as for the peoples of the Far East. We must attempt to enumerate and briefly describe them, for no survey of American operations in that part of the world can be intelligent or intelligible which does not take them into account. A fully logical arrangement is probably impossible; nor is much to be gained by separating those which issued out of the past from those which were novel.

One of the most obvious features and one of the most pressing problems of the Far East was the increasing pressure of population upon subsistence. We shall have occasion to note it as we pass from country to country. While it was more acute in some than in others, in almost all it constituted a nightmare for statesmen who did not try to dodge grim facts.

No one knew the exact population of China, which was almost certainly the largest block of people on the face of the earth, nor could anyone be certain whether it had been increasing during the twentieth century; but it probably had. It was clear that the pressure on the territories adjacent to China had mounted. We need only remind ourselves of the migration of millions of Chinese, in the first half of the twentieth century, into the heretofore relatively empty Manchuria, of the tensions between Mongols and Chinese in Inner Mongolia, of the influx of Chinese into British Malaya, in order to realize that the level of the reservoir must have risen. We know that in Japan the annual excess of births over deaths had been more than a million, that in Indonesia the total population rose from approximately sixty million in 1930 to more than seventy million in 1940 and probably seventy-five million in 1950, and that in India in the 1940's and the early 1950's it was mounting at the rate of more than a quarter of a million a month.

From this increase there was no prospect of early, and in most countries none even of distant, relief. Its causes were not altogether clear, but it had been in progress at least since the latter half of the nineteenth century. Ignorance and long-established custom prevented large-scale methods of population control except the tragically familiar ones of abortion, infanticide, war, pestilence, and famine. Nor was there much hope from indigenous leadership. Nearly everywhere the cry was heard that the three chronic evils were poverty, landlordism, and corruption. Here and there valiant spirits of trained intelligence were wrestling with the problem; but they were too few.

The pressure of population contributed to another major feature of the scene, a vast, swelling unrest. Years before, a thoughtful observer had described the problem of Japan as "a million more people each year, each of whom wants more things." True then, it was even more true in the postwar years, and not only in Japan. A deep-seated revolution was stirring among the underprivileged peoples not only of the Far East but also of most of the world. It arose from many causes. While one cause was the

28

pressure of population, another was ideas which had entered from the Occident. The ideas were brought not only by Communists, although they capitalized on the unrest. The unrest was there before the Communists became active in Asia. It arose partly because of the higher standard of living seen among the Westerners in Asia, reported by students or travelers in the Occident, pictured in the movies—many of them American—or heard of through other channels. It sprang primarily from the desire, native in the human spirit but usually imperfectly articulated, to reach out beyond present limitations to a larger and fuller life.

This revolutionary unrest was augmented by the breakdown of inherited cultures which had been in progress during part of the nineteenth and throughout the twentieth century, resulting from contact with the Occident. In the last four and a half centuries and especially during the last century and a half, the peoples of the Occident had spread all over the world. They brought with them their commerce, their machines, their ideas, and their culture. Primitive cultures quickly disintegrated. Higher civilizations, such as those of India, China, and Japan, were fairly resistant; but they were yielding, and that of China especially had been undergoing profound change. Early reconstruction and relative stability were unlikely. The collapse of the old cultures was accelerated by World War II and its accompaniments. Rapid transition, with high aspirations, frustrations, continued unrest, upheaval, rebellion, and here and there anarchy, was likely to be the story for generations to come.

Much of the unrest found a vent in nationalism. In part due to contagion from the West, nationalism fell onto fertile soil and met with eager response in the Far East. There it largely took the form of revolt against domination by peoples of the Occident. The restlessness had been mounting at least since the dawn of the twentieth century. It expressed itself in part and most spectacularly in efforts to throw off the political yoke of the Occident and took advantage of the weakening of the colonial powers of western Europe through two world wars. World War II, especially, was accompanied and followed by movements for full independence. In the aftermath of that struggle, India and Pakistan emerged, still members of the (formerly British) Commonwealth of Nations, but by their own choice and not under compulsion; Ceylon attained Dominion status; Burma became independent without even a formal tie with the Commonwealth; the Republic of Indonesia came into being; and in Indochina the French ostensibly granted autonomy and were battling to maintain even indirect control. The United States fulfilled an earlier promise and granted independence to the Philippines.

The desire for independence had more than political aspects. Nationalism was hypersensitive to any hint of other forms of imperialism. It objected to any attempt at economic domination. It was emphatic that transportation and industrial and commercial enterprises be either fully or predominantly in native hands. It might wish foreign capital to aid in the development of internal resources, but it insisted that the capital be completely free from any suspicion of foreign dictation. In missions and other cultural enterprises it demanded the end of every kind of foreign direction; and, while for a time financial assistance from abroad was accepted, any attempt at continuing supervision of the expenditure of that aid was resented. Foreign personnel might be received and even welcomed, but more and more they would have to be under the direction of domestic authorities.

With independence there came in some countries an access of hope and confidence. In contrast with the pessimism in western Europe and the chronic fear in the United States, thousands, especially among the articulate intelligentsia, had the exhilaration of believing that they were entering a new era of achievement. Emancipated from the domination of the Occident, so they were persuaded, they were free to embark on new enterprises for the development of their natural resources and were to obtain through industrialization the good things of life which machines had given the Occident, and which they had long envied.

However, to many of the more thoughtful, not only in the Occident but also in the Far East, a haunting doubt emerged. Could the peoples of the Far East, now under their own leaders, fully responsible for their own future, and no longer able to place on the Westerner the onus for their poverty, solve the basic problems presented by their teeming populations and by landlordism, poverty, and corruption? In India, Indonesia, and the Philippines comprehensive political unity was inherited from Occidental control. It had never been fully achieved under native rulers. The administrative machinery and the political institutions by which these areas were governed were the gifts of former rulers, importations and adaptions from the Occident. That was especially true of such devices as parliaments composed of elected representatives of the people, of the greater freedom of women, of the widely extended franchise, and of governments responsible to the electorate. In the west, where these processes of liberal democracy developed, they had never worked perfectly; but through the generations experience had been acquired, and among both the electorate and the elected a sense of responsibility had been developed, even though with dangerous gaps. Now that the Westerner's hand, to a considerable degree benevolent, had been withdrawn, could these newly independent peoples make the machinery work? That machinery had not arisen out of prolonged struggles and generations of trial and error.

Already there were indications of possible impending breakdown in India and the Philippines; and it was not clear that there was enough competent and honest leadership to effect successfully the transition from a colonial status and to make the required adjustments. Burma nearly collapsed after attaining independence, in no small degree because of the exigencies of the war years; and by 1951 recovery, while progressing, was not yet assured. A major cause of China's plight was the difficulty of working out institutions for the government of four hundred or four hundred and fifty million people, to fill the vacuum left by the collapse of the Confucian monarchy that had ruled the Chinese for more than two millenniums.

A major and urgent factor in the Far Eastern scene was the invasion of Russian Communism. Through Communism Russia had effected the most sobering incursion into the Far East which had thus far been seen. In several ways it was extraordinarily skillful. Communism had originated in western Europe and was largely worked out in London by a German, Karl Marx, but it was presented as non-Western and opposed to what the Far East had traditionally dreaded as Occidental imperialism. To those who knew history, it was clearly associated with the most recent stage of that Russian eastward drive which had been a persistent factor in the life of Asia since the late fifteenth century. Yet it was under indigenous leadership and purported to be a movement for the liberation of Asiatic peoples. This leadership did not think of itself as a tool of Russia. It appealed to nationalistic longings and scorned the charge that it was a Russian instrument. The tie with Russia was the more effective because it had been voluntarily assumed and was one of deep conviction. Communist propaganda, sincerely believed by many who spread it, presented Russia as leading the wave of the future and as the elder brother or disinterested friend of those who had been oppressed by Western capitalism and imperialism. The Communists of Asia, in accordance with the propaganda and direction emanating from Moscow, thought of themselves as sharing in a world revolution in which all peoples, including those of the United States, would be "liberated" and share in the golden age of a world-wide socialist order.

While masquerading under the name of democracy, Communist regimes were actually highly disciplined oligarchies, ruled despotically by a minority, the Communist Party. Like many oligarchies and monarchies before them, they professed to be government for the people; but, except by a diabolical twisting of words, they could not be called either of the people or by the people. The membership of the Party was carefully recruited, and its loyalty was assured by strict indoctrination, purges of the doubtful, and, in China, group examinations and self-criticism. Communism had a philosophy of the universe and of history which, under the specious guise of rationality, purported to be an inescapable conclusion from premises which were taught as axiomatic, to be understood but not questioned.

That philosophy was inculcated and held with the fanaticism of an infallible and dogmatic religious faith. It offered itself as the cure for the wrongs, and as the answer to the pent-up sense of injustice and the revolutionary longings, which were stirring the multitudes of the Far East. At the outset it was spread by propaganda which was not hampered by any regard for truth and would twist facts to serve its own purpose, balking at no expense. Armed force was only one of the tools of Communism, which virtuously presented itself as peace-loving and preferred to achieve its ends by methods short of war. When opponents blocked it in the use of those methods it regarded them as warmongers who left it no alternative to war. The Communist Party infiltrated its members into controlling positions in key organizations such as labor unions and student groups. By all the devices known to the printer and the artist it prepared its posters and cartoons to appeal to the illiterate or semiliterate masses. By slogans, catchy songs, and dances it won the multitudes. It addressed itself primarily to youth, seeking to capture the generation that was soon to be in power.

Yet the Russian use of Communism was the most dangerous invasion which the Far East had thus far known. The Russian

Communist leaders sought to make tools of the Far Eastern peoples. In this they seemed to be succeeding in China and North Korea, and thus among more millions than had ever been governed in the Far East from the West. Now and again there came reports of differences between the Russians and Chinese Communist leaders, but at least until the close of 1951 they were unproved. Those dominant in the Communist parties in China and Korea were following the Moscow line. Russian "advisers" appeared not to be popular with the masses of the Chinese, yet officially the "People's Republic" declared that Russia and the Russians were helping and not controlling them. Ultimately it would become clear that this "friendship" meant enslavement to a ruling group closely allied with Russia, and that the basic ills from which release had been so confidently promised, far from being removed, would in many cases be aggravated. Communism professed interest in the proletariat but was willing to liquidate millions of individuals for what it deemed the welfare of the whole.

The problem of the Far East was further aggravated by the tensions between Russia and the United States. The Korean War, caused by that tension, brought untold suffering to millions. The reciprocal hostility of the United States and Communist China led the latter to try to rid itself of persons supposed to sympathize with America. A third world war, fortunately not inevitable, in which the two giants would be the major contenders, would bring misery to peoples caught between them. Moreover, the victory of Communism in China, together with the American occupation of Japan, worked a striking change in the pre-1945 orientation of the United States. For years the United States had thought of China as a friend and Japan as an enemy. Now China became an enemy, and Japan a friend.

Still another complicating factor was the altered position of Japan. The collapse of Japan removed a menace to the freedom

of the peoples of the Far East. It also eliminated, at least for the
time being, a buffer and makeweight between Russia and the
United States. For years Japan had been more fearful of Russia
than of America. Russia was compelled to count on her as a traditional and serious enemy. Not only had the two fought in 1904–
1905, but they had had repeated armed clashes in the 1930's. Now
that Japan was down and disarmed, Russia and the United States
were scowling at each other across her prostrate body. Whether
Japan was an asset or a liability to the United States was not yet
clear. That she would recover eventually was probable. Whether
she would remain neutral and, if not, which side she would
espouse were by no means certain. To that question we must return later.

Moreover, from bitter and recent experience the other peoples
of the Far East had a profound fear of Japan. If and when Japan
recovered, might she not again become an aggressor? Quite un-
derstandably they looked with alarm upon the measures which
the United States was taking to put Japan on her feet, even
though its purpose was to lift a burden from the shoulders of the
American taxpayer, to enable the Japanese to raise their standard
of living from the sub-poverty level, to assist them to self-support
and self-respect, and so to obviate festering resentment and a
growing passion for revenge.

Western Europe was still an important factor in the Far Eastern scene. That was partly because what happened in western
Europe in large part shaped the policy of Russia and the United
States in the Far East, and partly because Europe needed Asian
raw materials and markets. Moreover, Great Britain, France, the
Netherlands, and Portugal retained territorial interests or claims
in the East. Of these only the British interest in Malaya and the
French in Indochina presented major difficulties in 1951; but
there was friction between the Netherlands and Indonesia, with
western New Guinea still a bone of contention.

Australia and New Zealand, especially Australia as the larger of the two and the nearer to Asia, had also to be reckoned with in the Far Eastern picture. Both had been participants in World War II. Australia had very narrowly escaped a Japanese invasion, and no major settlement of Far Eastern issues could well be attempted which failed to take her and her interests into consideration.

Of major importance in the Far East was the United Nations. Several of the countries of the Far East were members of that body, where their voices were often heard. The United Nations took a prominent part in the dispute between the Dutch and the Indonesians, in the conflict between Pakistan and India over Kashmir, and, above all, in Korea. Resistance to Communist aggression in Korea was carried on through the United Nations and in its name, and it was largely to save the United Nations from possible early demise that the United States undertook what proved to be the major share in opposing that aggression. Moreover, the question whether China should be represented in the United Nations by the Nationalists or by the Communists was a source of disagreement not only between the United States and Russia, but also between the United States on the one hand and India and Great Britain on the other.

The difficulties of American action in the Far East were enhanced by the way in which American foreign policy was formed. (To that intricate process we shall return in the next chapter and in later chapters.) Because of the many conflicting voices, the numerous agencies and bodies which had to be consulted, the pressures from interested power blocs, party rivalries, and domestic politics, decisions were often slow in being reached and at times appeared to contradict one another. Uncertainty was often the result, and foreign statesmen as well as foreign observers, in the Far East and elsewhere, were frequently mystified and looked upon the United States as unpredictable and undependable.

A further factor which cannot be too greatly stressed is that the Far East was not the only scene of the tension between the U.S.S.R. and the United States. American policy and action in that area were conditioned by other phases of the global contest. The European phase was of peculiar importance. Americans in high places were divided as to where major emphasis should be placed. Some, prominent among them General MacArthur, insisted that the battle was to be lost or won in the Far East. Others held that the primary concern of the United States must be in Europe. The latter contended that if western Europe, with its vast industrial equipment and potential, were seized by the Communists, the scales would tip, perhaps disastrously, against the United States and the free nations in favor of Russia and the Russian satellites. In general, this view prevailed. The major portion of American aid went toward the recovery and rearmament of Europe. To this was added the extensive American assistance to Greece and American concern for the situation in the Mediterranean and the Near East, intricately bound up with the defense of western Europe.

These, then, were the chief factors—some in the Far East and some outside that region—which confronted the United States after August, 1945, and which contributed to the shaping of its policies and actions.

Selected Bibliography

No one book quite covers the subject matter of this chapter. The one which most nearly does so is L. K. Rosinger and associates, *The State of Asia: A Contemporary Survey* (New York: Alfred A. Knopf, 1951). It is the most comprehensive survey which appeared between 1945 and 1952.

The subject is covered in brief summary in Chapter XVII of K. S. Latourette, *A Short History of the Far East,* rev. ed. (New York: Macmillan Co., 1951).

IV. DID THE UNITED STATES

HAVE A CONSISTENT,

COMPREHENSIVE POLICY?

DID THE UNITED STATES HAVE, AFTER AUGUST, 1945, a consistent, comprehensive policy for the Far East? Several persons with whom the plan for this book was discussed smiled or openly scoffed when that question was raised. To them the confusion and the endless debates in the Congress, on the public platform, in the press, and over the radio were so obvious an answer as to make even the query preposterous.

The seeming confusion was to be expected. It arose from the democratic process as Americans understand it. The traditional policy, which went under the name of the Open Door and had been either tacitly or explicitly accepted by almost all Americans for nearly half a century, had led the United States deep into the Far East and into commitments of a variety and magnitude which, even as late as 1941, few if any would have believed possible. What was to be done now? Discussion of the question was not carried on behind closed doors as it would have been under Communist rule or any other form of totalitarian regime; and decisions, when reached, were not handed down to be accepted, unchallenged, by the public. Rather, true to the American tradition, the discussion was conducted in public and through many channels. The result often appeared to be a woeful lack of decision and of consistency.

We can take space only to note these channels in the barest summary fashion. Under the Constitution and long practice the President has major but by no means sole responsibility for the conduct of foreign affairs. Yet Presidents have had so many other burdens that they have entrusted more and more of the work, even to the framing of policies, to their Secretaries of State. Of late years, moreover, the Department of State had necessarily attained large dimensions and had several divisions and other specialized branches. The Congress too, quite properly, concerned itself with foreign affairs. That was not only because of its constitutional responsibility for declaring war, but also because of its power over the purse, its obligation to raise and support armies, and its control of commerce, immigration, and naturalization. This was true of the Senate, which, under the Constitution, shares with the President the treaty-making power and the appointments to the major ranks of the diplomatic service, and of the House as well. The Congress insisted on a full share in discussing commitments and broad policies.

Inevitably foreign affairs entered into party politics, in spite of honest efforts at a bipartisan policy. In the years after August, 1945, many Republicans, some of them from sincere conviction that the Democratic administration had made grievous blunders, vigorously attacked existing policies and measures. Some demanded more aid to the Chinese Nationalist regime and declared that a "soft" attitude had been maintained toward the Communists. They insisted that the Communists be kept out of Formosa. In contrast, the economy bloc in Congress sought to reduce even such aid as was given.

The armed services, through the Department of Defense, often made their voices heard. While, fortunately, the American tradition has been that government policies are under civilian control, the advice of the services must be sought on what the United States needs for its defense, and on what military commitments it is in a position to undertake. The National Security Council, with representation from the armed services and the civilian element in the government, helped to coordinate civilian and military views.

The press and the news commentators joined in the discussion. Since World War I an increasing number of private associations and foundations had concerned themselves with international relations. They sought to provide the citizenry with data and to stimulate discussion for the development of an informed public opinion. Labor, business, and veterans' organizations also had a share in this process.

Under these circumstances, which Americans accept as part of the democratic process, although at times impatiently or somewhat wearily, views were expressed in great number and exhibited a wide variety and many contradictions. In the following chapters some of them will be mentioned and a few of the main controversies will be discussed.

Amid the multitude of conflicting voices and the necessities of a situation vastly more complex than that of the years before World War II, certain main features can be recognized. Basically, they arose either from the attempt to apply the principles underlying the Open Door policy or from the exigencies of the total world situation. This does not mean that the actions were always consistent with one another or with that policy, for they were not, or that mistakes were not made, for they were. It does mean that behind and through what looked like confusion the United States had a policy to which, with some deviations and modifications, it in general adhered. The effort was made to hold to certain principles.

One of these principles was the identity of the interests of the people of the United States with those of the peoples of Asia. In a notable speech in March, 1950, Secretary of State Acheson declared that the United States sought to aid the peoples of Asia "to achieve their own goals and ambitions in their own way." This obviously meant governments of their own choosing, sound administration, education, and development of their resources and technical skills to enable them to make a livelihood. Historically, the United States has wished other peoples, including those of the Far East, to have governments which they themselves could operate, which would not deprive them of their liberties, and which would not make them a menace to their neighbors. The United States has realized that these governments would not necessarily be patterned after its own, but might and probably would be quite different. What would promote the welfare of other peoples would promote the welfare of the American people, for, in the last analysis, what aids all aids each. These may seem to be platitudes, and they would be if they were not implemented. It was on ways and means to make them effective that judgments differed.

A second principle was the containment of Communism. This arose not from antagonism to the Russians as such but from a profound conviction that Communism was a major menace to the well-being not only of the people of the United States but also of peoples everywhere, including those of the Far East. Here there was a tragic clash of convictions, for thousands of Communists were equally sure that the United States and what it stood for constituted a major threat to the welfare of mankind. They were persuaded, moreover, that the United States was the champion of an order which was doomed, and that Communism, with Russia as its leading exponent, was the wave of the future. In this Americans were convinced that the Communists were completely in error, that their methods were diabolical, and that Communism meant the enslavement and misery of the peoples whom it dominated. Believing as they did, Americans sought to restrain the spread of Communism, both in the Far East and elsewhere.

This aim of containing Communism sometimes brought the United States into an unenviable position, for it seemed to make it the champion of regimes which it otherwise would not approve, or of which it had been very critical. That was notably the case

41

in Indochina. It was true of some aspects of the Nationalist government of China and might be paralleled in the Philippines. As we have said, Communists were extremely clever in presenting themselves as saviors from the palpable evils from which the peoples of the Far East suffered, and they concentrated on clamant injustices. Believing Communism to be a false messiah and seeking allies in the local scene to oppose it, the United States more than once found itself with strange bedfellows.

It must be added, lest the United States be thought to be the only country in such a compromising situation, that the U.S.S.R. also, by deliberate policy, worked with regimes which were not in accord with its aims. Thus it gave aid to Chiang Kai-shek in 1937–1939. During the early years of World War II, it aligned itself with imperialistic Japan. It was notably perfidious in its disregard of treaty obligations.

Another principle of the United States was that armed force would be employed to contain Communism whenever and wherever that seemed unavoidable. Thoughtful Americans realized that at best this was a clumsy method which did not reach the central problem, a problem primarily of rival ideologies, the ultimate test being which of the two in practice best served the highest welfare of the peoples of the world. Many Americans were of the opinion that their government in deed though not in theory relied too heavily upon the army, the navy, and aircraft. However, it must be noted that after August, 1945, the active use of armed force by the United States was principally in Korea, where American troops operated at the behest and under the direction of the United Nations, and in cooperation with the forces of other governments.

Moreover, in the effort to contain Communism, the United States by no means placed its only reliance upon its armed services. Its policy was not either-or, but both-and. It sought to help the peoples of the Far East to solve the problems which produced unrest, although the means employed, by their very nature, worked slowly and did not bring the quick returns promised by Communism. Until the Communists took over, the United States provided large financial subsidies for China. Through the Economic Cooperation Administration—ECA, to use the familiar alphabetical designation—it gave substantial aid in several crucial areas, including Korea, Formosa, Burma, Thailand, Indochina, and Indonesia, part of which went to projects in public health and agriculture. Through its information programs, largely by audiovisual aids and radio, ECA sought to familiarize the peoples of these areas with what it was doing and why. The Point Four Program, with broadly similar aims, emphasized technical assistance. Extensive aid was given through the government to bring students from these lands to educational institutions in the United States. The United States cooperated with the United Nations agencies which sought to promote the welfare of the Far East as of other parts of the world. For example, the International Bank for Reconstruction and Development, for which the United States provided a large proportion of the funds, advanced credits to India.

To offset Communist propaganda, the United States presented its case through the Voice of America—all too feebly subsidized, it was often said—and through the United States Information Service, operated through the Department of State, with staffs in various strategic centers.

Private American agencies also had a share in helping the peoples of the Far East to solve their basic problems. American capital investments in the region were not large. On the eve of World War II they were only about 4 per cent of all American assets abroad. Between a fifth and a third of this small total was in the Philippines, almost a third in Japan, and not quite a fifth in China. No accurate and comprehensive postwar figures seem to be available; but presumably, because of the political changes and unrest, the sum was less than in prewar years. American private capital had not even begun to provide what was judged necessary if the resources of the Far East were to be developed in a manner adequate to the needs of the population. In proportion to the population of the region, American trade was also very much less than in some other quarters of the globe. The long-cherished American dream of large-scale commerce and investment in the area had not been fulfilled. American business was reluctant to invest heavily in capital installations and commercial ventures in Far Eastern countries which were politically unstable and lay under the shadow of Communism. Also the Asian peoples were sensitive to the possibility of foreign economic domination. These factors tended to discourage hope that the needed help would come through this channel.

Some of the private foundations, notably that bearing the name of Rockefeller, had spent substantial sums in the Far East. After the war the Ford Foundation gave much attention to Asia. Christian missions from the United States, as we have said, were much more widespread and were of substantial assistance in education, medicine, public health, rural reconstruction, and spiritual and moral improvement. However, in their essential nature they were supranational and were not carried on for the purpose of furthering the ends of the United States. Through them much good will accrued to the United States; but any attempt to utilize what has been called this "reservoir" for purposes which even in the remotest degree could be suspected of furthering American "imperialism" would put in jeopardy both the missionaries and the indigenous Christian communities and institutions associated with them, thus nullifying much that had been accomplished. This unhappy fact was abundantly demonstrated in Japan and Korea on the eve of World War II and during the conflict, in China in the 1920's and again under Communist rule, and in North Korea after 1945. Indeed, it was because the Communists believed them to be tools of Western and American cultural imperialism that they took vigorous measures to terminate any semblance of a tie between Christian churches and institutions and Christians in the West.

Another principle on which the United States acted in the Far East after the summer of 1945 with a fair degree of consistency was regard for the effects of what it did in that region of the world upon western Europe. As we have already said, whether western Europe should have priority over the Far East was one of the subjects on which Americans were by no means fully agreed. Some influential Americans wished to commit the resources of the United States so extensively in the Far East that western Europe might have to take a decidedly secondary place. Yet beginning with World War II, when the European theater was accorded precedence over the Pacific and the Far East, the government of the United States held that western Europe was of greater importance. It believed that, in the policy of seeking to contain Communism, it was more important that western Europe, with its vast industrial equipment and its historic cultural ties with America, be kept out of Russian Communist hands than that Communism be expelled from its position in the Far East. It hoped that neither would need to be surrendered; but, if a choice were imperative, it held that the Far East and not western Europe should be sacrificed.

Still another concern of the United States in the Far East was the defence of its own territory. So far as that was possible, the United States sought to safeguard its borders from aggression. Where the outer bulwarks of that defense should be was in dispute. Some stoutly maintained that Japan, Okinawa, Formosa, and the Philippines were vital to American defense. Others felt that the United States did not need all these bases so far from its own shores.

A final principle on which the United States acted in the Far

East, as elsewhere, was that the obligations of membership in the United Nations must be fulfilled. More than any other one country, the United States was responsible for the existence of the United Nations. Imperfect though it was, the United Nations had the support of the majority of thoughtful Americans and their government. Wherever possible the United States acted and intended to continue to act through the U.N. and to support it. This seems to have been the deciding factor, although not the only one, in the determination to roll back the Communist invasion of South Korea. Had that aggression been permitted to go unchecked, so it was believed, the death knell of the United Nations would have been sounded. Memory was still vivid of the manner in which the failure of the League of Nations to stop Japan in her aggression in Manchuria had revealed its weakness and was an early sign of its demise.

These, then, were the main principles by which the United States governed its policies in the Far East in the six years after the defeat of Japan. We now turn to their application in specific countries and areas.

Selected Bibliography

V. M. Dean, *Main Trends in Postwar American Foreign Policy* (New York: Institute of Pacific Relations and Oxford University Press, 1950).

U.S. Technical and Economic Assistance in the Far East (Washington: Mutual Security Agency, 1952).

The United States in World Affairs, 1945–47, 1947–48, 1948–49, 1949, and 1950. A series published for the Council on Foreign Relations by Harper & Brothers, New York.

S. Jenkins, *Trading with Asia* (New York: American Institute of Pacific Relations, 1946).

A. R. Miller, "American Investments in the Far East," *Far Eastern Survey*, Vol. XIX, No. 9 (May 3, 1950).

v. INDIA AND PAKISTAN

WITH PREWAR INDIA, INCLUDING WHAT IS NOW INDIA and Pakistan, the United States traditionally had relatively little contact. American trade and investments were slight. American Protestant missionaries were about as numerous as missionaries from the British Isles and were found in most parts of the subcontinent, initiating and conducting various cultural enterprises, chiefly churches, schools, and hospitals. During World War II India became a staging area for the air lift to China and for campaigns in Burma, and a fairly large number of American troops were stationed there; the United States also assisted India's defense effort. However, aside from minorities in church circles which supported missionaries, Americans knew little of India and were only vaguely conscious of its existence.

So far as they had an opinion, Americans were inclined to favor Indian aspirations for independence. But the government of the United States did not wish to embarrass the British government, at a time when the two were closely associated in war and the latter was fighting with its back to the wall, by urging more autonomy. To be sure, in 1942 President Roosevelt suggested to Prime Minister Churchill the establishment of provisional Dominion status for India as a means of making the Indians more cooperative in helping to bring about the defeat of Japan. An American representative, Colonel Louis Johnson, participated in the Cripps negotiations, through which the British attempted unsuccessfully to bring about an amicable settlement with the Indian nationalists, who were determined to use the occasion of the war to constrain Britain to grant full independence. Moreover, William Phillips, in India with the rank of Ambassador, felt that the military position of the United States in India entitled it to a voice in the negotiations, for upon their success might hinge the fate of the war in that part of the world. During the war, British and Indian troops shared in Lend-Lease supplies. In June and July, 1945, American diplomacy had a part in obtaining the release from prison of some of the Indian leaders. Yet the United States was reluctant to seem to be trespassing in the British Empire.

After the defeat of Japan, in the autumn and winter of 1946, when negotiations for independence were being troubled by the differences between the Indian National Congress and the Muslim League, the government of the United States, through Acting Secretary of State Acheson, formally expressed its hope of "a peaceful transition to complete freedom." In February, 1947, Secretary of State Marshall voiced a similar concern. Even before independence, at the time when the control of foreign affairs passed largely into Indian hands, the United States was quick to establish diplomatic relations, thus welcoming the step toward full nationhood. In 1946 the diplomatic missions in Washington and New Delhi were raised to the status of embassies, and before August, 1947, an Indian Ambassador had been received in Washington and an American Ambassador in New Delhi.

In 1947 independence was achieved on a basis of partition, and two new states, India and Pakistan, took their places in the family of nations. India was by far the larger. It comprised nearly 350,000,000 people, approximately a fifth of the population of the world. It therefore became somewhat more prominent in world affairs. Born of intense nationalism, India wished to play a role in Asia and in the world commensurate with her size and her great cultural heritage. Her representatives took an important part in the deliberations of the United Nations. Her leaders wished her to avoid entanglement in the struggle between the Communist bloc led by Russia and the free nations led by the United States.

Yet the leaders of India were more sympathetic with the free nations; and, as was natural because of the long British connection, her political institutions were more nearly akin to those of Great Britain and the United States than to those of Russia. Moreover, there were close economic ties between India and Britain. When Britain through its Labor government took the initiative in constraining the Hindus and Muslims to arrange their differences, and eventually herself cut the Gordian knot which had delayed the achievement of independence, the British became popular in India, eventually more so than the Americans. Although she chose to become a republic, India voluntarily remained in the Commonwealth with the King as its symbol. Indians looked with interest upon what was taking place in Russia; but, in spite of a small but active and sometimes extremely troublesome Communist Party in their midst, as a whole they had no great fear of Russia or of Communism.

Probably there was more fear and therefore more dislike of the United States than of Russia. Because of past experiences which they had bitterly resented, Indians intensely disliked anything that even remotely smacked of Western imperialism. They envied and feared the wealth and the power of the United States. They wanted financial assistance in the development of their national resources and their industries, but only on terms which would not in the slightest degree compromise their full economic and political autonomy. The role, especially the recent role, of the United States in the Far East made many Indians regard it as a champion of imperialism.

On several issues tension arose between India and the United States. One of these was Indonesia, to which we shall revert later. India, having won her freedom, wished to champion the other Asian peoples who sought emancipation from foreign rule. She was therefore critical of the attempts of the Dutch to reestablish themselves in Indonesia. The Indian government particularly resented the use of Indian troops by the British in Indonesia, during the interim between the defeat of Japan and the arrival of Dutch forces, and viewed with suspicion American action or lack of action that might seem to favor the Dutch. But when the Indonesian question came up in the United Nations India and the United States were usually not far apart.

Far more thorny was the issue of Kashmir. This was a large princely state which under the British had been semiautonomous in domestic affairs, and which both India and Pakistan desired to incorporate. The Hindu Maharajah officially acceded to India. India regarded his action as legal and binding, and believed that it would be supported by the people under the pro-Indian Muslim leader, Sheik Abdullah, although the majority of the population were Muslim. Pakistan not unnaturally believed that if a fair plebiscite were held the popular vote would favor accession to the Muslim neighbor. The irruption of Pakistani tribesmen, intent upon winning Kashmir for Pakistan, inflamed Indian public opinion. War between India and Pakistan seemed imminent, especially because Kashmir was added to other issues causing friction between the two countries.

Some Americans in high places took a particularly grave view of the situation, for Kashmir was in the northwest not far from the path by which a Russian invasion had traditionally been feared, and the weakening of one or both belligerents might give the U.S.S.R. an excuse for intervention. At the instance of India the Security Council of the United Nations tried to settle the dispute, without success by 1951. The United States assumed the leading role in seeking to compose the quarrel, and an American was appointed mediator by the United Nations. America was blamed by both Indians and Pakistanis for not having brought about a decision favorable to their cause.

A less important issue on which India and the United States differed was Hyderabad, another large princely state, with a predominantly Hindu population but with a Muslim ruler, the

Nizam. The Nizam wished to remain as nearly independent as possible, but India insisted that he accede to the Indian Union. In September, 1948, the Nizam asked the President of the United States to aid in settling the dispute, but was told that the request should come from both sides. Not long thereafter the Indian army entered Hyderabad. In the United Nations the United States took the position that India was in the wrong in using armed force, and the Security Council voted to give Hyderabad a hearing. This was a defeat for India; but the next day Hyderabad surrendered, and no major friction with the United States developed.

In 1950–1951 the question of food relief from the United States to India assumed importance. The problem of feeding India's millions, always chronic and aggravated by the continued increase in population and the distressing inflation, became particularly acute because of drought. It was proposed that the United States government make a gift to India of 2,000,000 tons from its store of surplus wheat. The project was urged by many philanthropic and church groups in the United States and by President Truman. But action by the Congress was delayed, partly by the congested state of the legislative calendar, partly by the disapproval of many Congressmen for India's attitude toward the U.S.S.R. and Communist China, and partly by disagreement as to the form the grant should take. Should it be an outright gift or a loan? If the latter, what should be the terms? Should the grant be made conditional upon repayment by India with products needed in the defense program of the United States? The long delay was a source of irritation in India and counteracted much of whatever good will might have been attained by prompt action.

The situation was made more embarrassing by promises of food from Russia and Communist China—neither on anything approaching the scale proposed from the United States—but given in a manner which furthered kindly feelings for these countries in

India. Nor was the tension substantially eased by relief from private American sources or by the Point Four Agreement reached late in 1950 between India and the United States for technical assistance to a value of $1,200,000 in agriculture, river valley development, and transportation. However, early in the summer of 1951 the necessary Congressional action was taken and a food loan of $190,000,000 was granted. In anticipation of the arrival of the first shipload of grain late in July, the government of India increased its per capita allowance of grain.

Other sources of friction arose over race. Indians were critical of the status of Negroes in the United States. They resented, too, what they felt to be the tendency of the United States to support South Africa on the moot question, on which Indians had long been highly sensitive and on which the Indian government took an outspoken stand, of the treatment of Indians in that country.

What in some ways was the most serious difference between India and the United States, in the six years after the surrender of Japan, developed over China. India, along with Burma, withdrew recognition from the Chinese Nationalist regime in December, 1949, and accorded it to that of the Communists. In this she was soon followed by Great Britain and several other European governments. If enough members concurred, that would entail permitting the Communist government to take China's seat in the United Nations. From this, however, as we are to see at length later, the United States was in dissent. It continued to regard the Nationalist regime as the legitimate government of China and supported its claim to speak for that country in the United Nations.

In the Korean War which broke out in June, 1950, India attempted the role of mediator. She voted for the Security Council resolution of June 25 which brought the United Nations actively into that struggle, but her Prime Minister, Nehru, quickly expressed the wish of his government that it might "be possible to

put an end to the fighting and to settle the dispute by mediation."
Moreover, India abstained from voting on the Security Council
resolution of June 27, which recommended that "the members of
the United Nations furnish such assistance to the Republic of
Korea as may be necessary to repel the armed attack and to restore international peace and security in the area." On July 13
Nehru, in a note to President Truman and in a similar message
to Premier Stalin, proposed that representatives of the (Communist) People's Republic of China be seated in the Security
Council so that Russia, China, and the United States, "with the
help and cooperation of other peace-loving nations," might find
a basis for terminating the conflict. Stalin quickly agreed. But
Washington replied that the United States did not believe "the
termination of the aggression from Northern Korea" should "be
contingent in any way upon the determination of other questions
which are currently before the United Nations"; and that "the
decision between competing claimant governments for China's
seat in the United Nations is one which must be reached by the
United Nations on its merits."

The United States continued to oppose the admission of Communist China to the United Nations, holding that the Nationalist
government was the legitimate representative of China, while
India and several other countries felt that the danger of war was
increased by keeping the Communist government outside the
U.N. India opposed the crossing of the 38th parallel by the U.N.
forces in Korea, and even after the Chinese Communist intervention in Korea she continued to seek a negotiated settlement of the
Korean War whenever an opportunity to do so arose.

Late in 1950 the invasion or "liberation" of Tibet, an autonomous dependency of China on India's border, alarmed some sections of Indian opinion; but the Indian government remained officially friendly to Communist China, while the United States became even more hostile after the Chinese intervention in Korea.

Thus, although the autumn of 1951 found India and the United States still on friendly terms, there were points of strain which disturbed observers in both countries. Indian public opinion tended to regard the United States with something of the dislike and fear which had once been directed toward Great Britain, while most Americans felt that India's attitude toward the menace of Communism was unrealistic. India refused to sign the American-sponsored peace treaty with Japan, chiefly because it permitted American troops to be stationed in Japan after peace was concluded, made possible a United States trusteeship over the Ryukyu and Bonin islands (which India thought should be returned to Japan), and failed to provide for the return of Formosa to China. India's position did not ease the relations between herself and the United States.

In 1951, however, Indian-American relations took a turn for the better with the appointment of a new American Ambassador, Chester Bowles, and early in 1952 an agreement was signed under which the United States would grant about $50,000,000 from Mutual Security Act funds for technical cooperation in India's economic development.

Selected Bibliography

L. K. Rosinger, *India and the United States* (New York: Macmillan Co., 1950).

For developments after the completion of Rosinger's book see *The United States in World Affairs, 1950,* by R. P. Stebbins and the Research Staff of the Council on Foreign Relations (New York: Harper & Brothers, 1951).

VI. SOUTHEAST ASIA:

A RECENT AMERICAN HEADACHE

IN THIS CHAPTER WE ARE GROUPING SEVERAL COUN-
tries together, though not because they are identical in culture,
ethnic composition, or history—for they display a wide variety.
But they form a distinct geographical region, and they all, except
Thailand, have one common characteristic: until World War II
they were colonies of western European powers, and after that
conflict they emerged from colonial status or were moving in that
direction. These countries are Burma, Malaya, Thailand (Siam),
Indochina, and Indonesia. The Philippines might be included,
for geographically and racially they are a northern extension of
the Indonesian archipelago. However, because of their history,
culture, and peculiar relations with the United States, they must
be reserved for a separate chapter.

During the Japanese occupation the former European possessions had a taste of autonomy, for the Japanese encouraged what
they termed independence and carried on intense propaganda
against Western imperialism. This gave the peoples of the region
a release from white domination and strengthened opposition to
the return of European rule. In the hiatus after the collapse of
Japanese power before European colonial regimes could attempt
to resume control, all had experience in self-government.

Before World War II American interests in southeast Asia
varied from country to country. In Burma, Thailand, and Indochina American investments were negligible. They were somewhat larger in Indonesia and British Malaya, because of petroleum in the former, tin in the latter, and rubber in both. Yet they
were not as substantial as in China, Japan, or the Philippines; and,

55

all told, they were only a small percentage of the total foreign holdings of Americans. British Malaya was important to the United States as a main source of tin and rubber. The prosperity of the colony, which had soared since the advent of the automobile, was to no small degree dependent upon the American market. Americans predominated in the Protestant missions in Burma, Thailand, and Indochina, and had a share in Protestant missions in British Malaya; but almost no American missionaries were to be found in Indonesia. Politically, the United States had displayed little interest in the area, even though treaty relations with Thailand had begun as early as 1833.

After the outbreak of World War II in Europe and especially after the German occupation of the Netherlands and France, American interest in southeast Asia increased. The partial power vacuum left by the weakening of these two countries tempted Japan to move southward. The United States made it increasingly clear that it would oppose any attempt by the Japanese to take possession of Malaya or Indonesia. It was in this region rather than at Pearl Harbor that President Roosevelt and his advisers expected the issue to be joined and the blow to fall. After Pearl Harbor, the United States suffered some severe reverses in the effort to defend Indonesia against the Japanese, for its aid to the beleaguered Dutch was "too little and too late."

Following the defeat of Japan, American interest in the region continued. For this there were at least three reasons. The United States was concerned to see the aspirations of the peoples of the area for independence realized. Thus, incidentally, the suspicions and fears of many of the British, Dutch, and French were aroused and confirmed. The United States also wished to prevent Communism from taking over the region. Indeed, it was opposed to any enemy, potential or actual, coming into possession of this rich and strategic area. Then, too, southeast Asia was of economic importance to the United States, both directly and through triangular trade. Much of the tin, rubber, and petroleum produced in the area was sold in the United States, largely through the British and Dutch. It thus became the source of American exchange to a dollar-hungry part of the world in whose economic stability the United States had a strong stake in the struggle with Communism. After the Communists conquered China, American interest in bolstering southeast Asia rapidly mounted.

Burma

During World War II Burma entered prominently into the consciousness of the American people as the terminus of the "Burma Road" which afforded a means of access to the part of China not occupied by the Japanese. There Americans shared in the defeat administered to the British. Americans were deeply concerned in the efforts to reopen a route to China by way of Burma.

The Japanese granted Burma a species of independence. It was partly spurious, but the Burmese were accorded much leeway in the administration of their domestic affairs. They organized peasant unions and cooperatives and gained military experience both in cooperation with the Japanese and in underground resistance to them.

After the expulsion of the Japanese the British attempted to restore their rule in Burma, with the promise of an early grant of Dominion status. That, however, did not satisfy the Burmese, and the British position became more and more untenable. Early in 1947 the Labor government in Westminster took steps to give Burma independence, inside or outside the British Commonwealth. The Burmese elected to leave the Commonwealth; and in January, 1948, a treaty with Great Britain came into force in which the latter recognized Burma as "a fully independent sovereign State."

Independence did not bring internal peace. Several parties,

among them two varieties of Communists, contended for power. Civil war threw the land into disorder, and the situation was aggravated by strife between the Karens, the largest minority, and the national government, run largely by the dominant group, the Burmese. By the latter part of 1951 peace and order were gradually being restored; but Communism was still a menace, especially since it was now in control of China, on the northern border. Burmese Communists, although divided, operated as guerrillas and hoped eventually to take over the country.

The contacts of the United States with the new Burma were not extensive. The United States officially recognized the Rangoon government. It feared that Burma would fall to the Communists. These forebodings were not allayed by the fact that Burma was the first non-Communist country to give official recognition to the People's Republic of China (December 17, 1949). Moreover, Burma supported the People's Republic in its demand for China's seat in the United Nations. Although these actions could be explained in part by the nearness of Communist China and the desire not to provoke that power, they did not promote friendship with the United States.

On January 12, 1950, Secretary of State Acheson said that neither London, Washington, Paris, nor The Hague could determine what the policies of the new nations in southeast Asia were to be, for these peoples were "proud of their new national responsibility." Yet he hinted that the United States would be willing to help, but "only when the conditions are right for help to be effective." The next day, as if in reply, the Burmese Ambassador at Washington pointedly said that "there should be no talk of military aid" to Asian countries unless that aid were requested, and declared that the smaller Asian countries did not wish to be shuttlecocks between the two hostile camps. In April, 1950, a mission headed by R. Allan Griffin, sent by the United States to southeast Asia to prepare the way for such technical assistance as the Congress might vote to offer to that region, visited Rangoon. By the autumn of 1950 the Economic Cooperation Administration had a special technical and economic mission in Burma, and an agreement was signed by which it was expected that Burma would receive from eight to ten million dollars during 1951. This was for the purpose of helping Burma solve her basic economic problems and quiet the unrest upon which Communism fed.

British Malaya

When World War II reached the Far East, the lower part of the Malay Peninsula was under British rule. Most of the mainland was governed indirectly through Malay rulers. What were known as the Straits Settlements, of which the most important unit was the island of Singapore, were administered as a Crown colony. The population was conglomerate. The two largest elements, in 1941 about equal in size, were the Malays and the Chinese. The Malays, who had been there longer, predominated on the mainland. The Chinese, whose members had greatly increased by immigration in the twentieth century, were particularly prominent in Singapore, the largest city. There was a substantial Indian contingent. The British, a small minority, were the governing group. As we have said, in the twentieth century before the Japanese occupation, the area had been very prosperous mainly because of its exports of tin and rubber.

In what to many in the outside world seemed an amazingly short time after their full-scale attack launched in December, 1941, the Japanese took Malaya, including Singapore. During the years of the Japanese occupation, the Chinese were a center of disaffection. From them had come much financial support for Nationalist China, with which the Japanese were at war. They were now constrained by the Japanese to make large contributions to Japan's war chest. It was chiefly among the Chinese, aided by a few Indians and fewer Malays, that organized resistance to the Japanese developed. This was spearheaded by Chinese Communists and took the form of bands of guerrillas which constituted the Anti-Japanese Army.

The defeat of Japan was followed by the reestablishment of British rule. Important modifications were made by the British in their administration of the region. These gave rise to some dissatisfaction and were later modified. Economic conditions were bad immediately after the war, and the Malayan Communist Party sought to capitalize on the resulting unrest. Following a pattern of Communist effort which appeared also in other countries, they attempted to form a coalition of the opponents of the existing government, with themselves safely although not at first obviously in control. In 1948 the Communists launched a revolt with the purpose of making rule costly for the British and cowing the conservative Chinese. The revolt was suppressed, and many non-Communists who had cooperated fell away. Nevertheless armed guerrillas under Communist leadership continued an active campaign of robbery and terrorism which, at the end of 1951, the British had not yet been able to suppress.

As before World War II, so after that struggle, the prosperity of Malaya was largely dependent upon the American market, chiefly for rubber but also for tin. In its need for dollars to recoup its war-ravaged economy, Britain sought to tighten its control over Malaya's trade and industry and to channel their American earnings to London. This was especially important, because 16 per cent of all the British Commonwealth's shipments to the United States in 1948 were from Malaya. This dictation from Britain gave rise to criticism in Malaya, especially from the Chinese, for they were deeply involved in the region's industry and exports and had no patriotic loyalties which would make them acquiesce in measures to aid British recovery.

Irritation in Malaya against the United States was furthered by the development of the American synthetic rubber industry and of Texan tin smelting. This development was, it need scarcely be said, an attempt to fill the gap produced by the cutting off of supplies from Malaya during the Japanese occupation. After the war, the United States government continued to subsidize the production of synthetic rubber, thereby reducing the price that the Malayan producers could charge in competition, and required American manufacturers to use specific proportions of the synthetic product. In 1948 the American Congress further disappointed Malayan hopes by continuing governmental control until 1950 and setting the production of synthetic rubber at a minimum of 221,000 tons a year. It might soon total 1,000,000 tons a year. All this, so Malayan interests complained, reduced the price of rubber below their costs of production. So, too, the producers of Malaya's tin wished the United States to end its subsidy to the Texan smelters and to pay a higher price for the metal. However, American domestic competition in tin was not so serious a menace as synthetic rubber, and in 1949 Malaya was producing almost as much of the metal as before the war.

Thailand (Siam)

Thailand, or Siam, the one country in southeast Asia which remained independent of European rule, managed to maintain the semblance of that status during World War II. It did so under the guise of an alliance with Japan and the other Axis powers. During the war a Free Thai movement sought to counter Japan and gave valuable aid to her enemies. However, after the outbreak of hostilities between Japan on the one hand and Great Britain and the United States on the other, Thailand formally declared war on the latter two countries. Great Britain retaliated by a declaration of war on Thailand, but the United States did not do so.

After the defeat of Japan, Great Britain made sweeping demands on Thailand as a condition of restoring friendly relations, and the Anglo-Thai treaty of January 1, 1946, incorporated some of them. Pressure from the United States caused Great Britain to make radical modifications in the treaty in the direction of leniency.

The United States was consistently friendly to Thailand. It recognized all the postwar governments. It aided Thailand in gaining prompt entry to the United Nations, supported it in maintaining its independence and territorial integrity, and facilitated foreign technical and financial assistance in accomplishing its postwar rehabilitation, but without jeopardizing its autonomy. In 1950, $11,000,000 was recommended for this last purpose through the Economic Cooperation Administration, and a military assistance agreement was concluded between Thailand and the United States, with the expectation that the equipment provided by the latter would be used to reenforce Thai defense on the Indochinese border. Postwar Thailand was prosperous through exports of tin and rubber, which were purchased mainly by the United States. Thailand was also important to the United States because as a rice-exporting country it reduced the food deficit in some other portions of east and southeast Asia and thus lessened the unrest which might give opportunity for the growth of Communism. Thailand followed the American lead and sent a contingent of troops to fight in Korea.

Indochina

In Indochina the story is more complicated; and the effort by the United States to contain Communism involved it more deeply than in Burma, Malaya, or Thailand. Yet before World War II the United States had been little concerned with the area.

It will be recalled that at the outbreak of World War II Indochina was under French rule and protection. French interest dated from near the end of the eighteenth century, having come largely in connection with French Roman Catholic missions. The French conquest began in the third quarter of the nineteenth century and was completed in the 1880's. At the time France became involved in World War II Indochina was made up of Tonkin, Annam, and Cochin China, along the eastern and southern coastal plains, inhabited predominantly by the Vietnamese and with a tradition of political unity; Cambodia, quite distinct culturally and historically; and Laos, a thinly peopled region in the northwest. The Vietnamese constituted about three-fourths of the population of Indochina. Cochin China was governed directly as a colony with a representative in the French Chamber of Deputies in Paris. Tonkin and Annam were protectorates. The fiction of indirect government was maintained in Annam under an emperor. Cambodia was a protectorate under a native monarch. In Laos there was a kingdom whose ruler was continued, but much of the area was directly under French administration.

Vietnamese educated in France became acquainted with democracy, and some of them were committed to left-wing ideas. In the 1920's Ho Chi Minh, a Vietnamese who had been active in France as a Socialist and Communist and had had more than a year in Moscow, established himself at Canton and organized the Vietnam Revolutionary Youth League, from which members went to Indochina to stimulate revolutionary cells. He then went to Hong Kong and there founded the Indochinese Communist Party, which gained a few adherents among the Vietnamese intelligentsia and peasants. There was also a non-Communist Vietnam Nationalist Party, modeled after the Kuomintang in China. In 1930–1931 both Communist and non-Communist attempts to overthrow French rule were suppressed.

After the fall of France in 1940, the Japanese gradually extended their control over Indochina. Theoretically the French remained in power, but only with Japanese permission; and in March, 1945, the Japanese unseated what survived of the French regime. Their control was complete. To aid them they recalled Bao Dai, the former Emperor of Annam, who had abdicated. He proclaimed the independence of the empire, gave it the old name of Vietnam, and united under it Annam and Tonkin. Under Japanese pressure, the King of Cambodia declared his independence, as did also a king in Laos.

Vietnamese nationalists were divided in their attitude toward Bao Dai. Some refused to support him, for they regarded him as a puppet of Japan. Others cooperated with him and thus gained experience in self-rule. Revolutionaries gathered in southern China, near the Indochinese border, and were organized by Ho Chi Minh into the Vietnam Independence League, best known as the Viet Minh. In addition a Chinese-sponsored Vietnamese Independence League also functioned abroad. Partly to worry the Japanese and partly to extend its own influence in Indochina, the Kuomintang under Chiang Kai-shek aided both leagues.

Before the Japanese collapse the Viet Minh, under Ho Chi Minh's leadership, set up the framework of a government for the entire country, the Democratic Republic of Vietnam. In August, 1945, Bao Dai abdicated his phantom throne. In September, 1945, the Viet Minh proclaimed the independence of the Democratic Republic of Vietnam. That regime claimed authority over Tonkin, Annam, and Cochin China. It governed the country, preserved peace and order, and maintained the public services. In it both Communists and non-Communists were represented. Vietnamese nationalists later pointed to it as proof that they were quite competent to administer the land without French aid.

In pursuance of a decision of the Potsdam Conference, British and Chinese troops were sent to disarm the Japanese and free the Allied prisoners. The British operated south of the sixteenth parallel; and the Chinese, north of that line. The British in their zone, which included Cambodia and Cochin China, enabled the French to reestablish themselves, for so they interpreted their mission. North of the sixteenth parallel, the Chinese permitted the Ho Chi Minh regime to continue and hoped to gain control of the new Republic. Ho Chi Minh drew into his government some non-Communists from other nationalist groups and clearly had the support of the majority in both the Anglo-French and the Chinese zones. In February, 1946, the Chinese entered into an agreement with the French by which they withdrew in return for important concessions by the latter, mostly of French privileges in China and recognition of the rights of the large Chinese population in Indochina.

In March, 1946, the French recognized the Democratic Republic of Vietnam as a "free state . . . forming part of the Indochinese Federation and the French Union," and in return the French army was permitted to come back but was to leave by 1952. The French also had formal understandings with Cambodia and Laos. Partly from fear of the United States, which they suspected of aiming to put Indochina under international trusteeship, the French had evolved a plan for an Indochinese Federation. While still under French supervision, it was to have more economic and administrative autonomy than had existed before the Japanese occupation.

However, fighting broke out between the French and the Democratic Republic of Vietnam, partly because there were radically different conceptions of what constituted a free state, and partly because many French wished to restore their position to what it had been before 1940. In 1948 certain Vietnamese elements, at the instance of the French, set up a rival government and induced Bao Dai to head it, thus hoping to attract moderate Vietnamese nationalists. However, very few of the latter were willing to serve. The regime headed by Ho Chi Minh claimed full independence, and the French carried on a confused war with its armies.

The Indochinese struggle had wide implications. The French were reluctant to yield, partly because they professed distrust of the ability of the Vietnamese to govern themselves, and partly because they feared that the grant of full independence would be followed by demands for similar concessions in their possessions in North Africa. Early in 1950 the Ho Chi Minh regime, the Democratic Republic of Vietnam, usually known as Viet Minh, was recognized as fully independent by Russia and her satellites, including Communist China. Their triumph in China brought the Chinese Communists to the Indochinese border, and the Communist threat to all southeast Asia was greatly increased. In February, 1950, Yugoslavia recognized Viet Minh. Partly to offset the Viet Minh menace, in 1950 France gave a larger measure of autonomy to Vietnam, Laos, and Cambodia, while still holding them in the French Union.

Indochina presented a perplexing problem to the United States, which by tradition looked with favor upon the aspirations of subject peoples for freedom. There were Americans, including some in the Department of State, who wished to bring pressure on France to grant full independence to Indochina, or at least to Vietnam. They believed that if this were done promptly the moderates among the nationalists would be able to control the government and keep the Communists out of power. They held that the longer the step was delayed, the more moderates would be driven into the arms of the Communists. On the other hand, there were those who, with wry faces and very reluctantly, believed that the United States should support the French, and this became the prevailing view; but they devoutly hoped that the latter would yield to moderate Vietnamese views and move rapidly toward the grant of much greater autonomy. They were moved by the desire to contain Communism, for they feared that the defeat of the French would mean the triumph of the Viet Minh regime and the loss of another bulwark against the Communist sweep across southeast Asia. They also hesitated to complicate conditions in France, for the political situation there was unstable and a false step might throw the government into the hands of either De Gaulle on the one extreme or the Communists on the other.

In general, the government of the United States supported the French, but went as far as it dared toward urging greater concessions. It welcomed the granting of increased autonomy to Vietnam, Cambodia, and Laos, and significantly raised its consulate general in Saigon to the rank of a legation.

The victory of Communism in China and the recognition of the Ho Chi Minh regime by the Soviet Union, its satellites, and the People's Republic of China led Secretary of State Acheson to say (February, 1950) that these acts revealed "Ho in his true colors as the mortal enemy of native independence in Indochina" and the instrument of Russian-Communist tyranny. On February 2, 1950, the French government ratified its agreements with the Bao Dai regime, but not until after a violent debate in the French Assembly. When that act made it clear that France was prepared to stand by Bao Dai, the United States and Great Britain hastened (February, 1950) to accord their formal recognition to his government.

The United States also provided military aid in the fight against Ho Chi Minh. The French were apprehensive that this might be the precursor to American economic inroads and also were alarmed by the American opposition to colonialism. Accordingly, the commander of the French forces in Indochina insisted that American military equipment be given only to the French and not to the Bao Dai government. He had no confidence in the stability of the French-stimulated Bao Dai regime. Yet in May, 1950, Secretary Acheson said that the United States would grant military and economic aid to restore security and develop "genuine nationalism" in Indochina, and that this would go not only to the

French but also to each of the associated states in that area. Actually assistance was channeled entirely through the French. After war broke out in Korea, President Truman announced "acceleration in the furnishing of military assistance to the forces of France and the associated states in Indochina and the dispatch of a military mission to provide close working relations with these forces."

In the autumn of 1950 the Viet Minh forces made decided gains against the French, and the Premier of Bao Dai's government demanded complete independence. In 1951 the situation was still none too hopeful for the United States. The slowness of the French in meeting the demands of the non-Communist Vietnamese nationalists (although they said they were turning over the responsibilities of government to the native regimes as rapidly as the latter were able to assume them), the weakness of the Bao Dai regime, the unwillingness of Vietnamese nationalists to support it, the gains of Viet Minh, and the aggressive Communism across the border in China were all unpropitious. India, Pakistan, Burma, and Indonesia, hostile as they were to colonialism, were cool toward the French-sponsored structures.

Indonesia

Indonesia is by far the largest of the lands of southeast Asia, in both area and population. In 1951 it had an estimated population of seventy-five million, or more than the combined populations of all the other countries which we have classified under southeast Asia. Significantly, that represented an increase from sixty million, or 25 per cent, since 1930. About two-thirds were on Java. Although not the largest in the archipelago, that island was therefore predominant in the political life of the area.

Such unity as Indonesia possessed was partly due to Dutch rule. While in one form or another Malay was spoken by the majority,

68

linguistic, racial, cultural, and religious diversity existed; and never had any one regime brought as large a proportion of the islands under one administration as the Dutch. Although the Dutch had gained their first footholds in the seventeenth century, most of their expansion in point of area had been comparatively recent, in the nineteenth and twentieth centuries. Even then not all the archipelago was acquired, for parts of Timor and Borneo remained under the British and the Portuguese. The amalgamation into one nation was very incomplete.

Yet, as elsewhere in southeast Asia, nationalism developed. It was particularly strong among the intelligentsia who had been educated in Europe, and who there had imbibed it at its source. The Dutch made some concessions to it between World War I and World War II, but continued to hold the controlling hand. Nationalism took several forms: religious, basing itself on Islam, the faith professed by the majority; moderate, willing to move slowly, in cooperation with the Dutch, toward independence; radical, demanding immediate independence; and Marxist, aiming at a revolutionary workers' state. The division among the nationalists complicated the years after 1945 and had to be taken into consideration by the United States in its Indonesian policies.

Japanese rule brought a marked stimulus to the demand for independence. As elsewhere, the Japanese issued propaganda directed against Western imperialism. They encouraged the setting up of a professedly independent government which would cooperate with them. Most Indonesian nationalist leaders took posts under the Japanese. The Japanese occupation stimulated the drive toward autonomy.

After the Japanese collapse, the Dutch endeavored to come back. Indonesia had been closely tied to the Dutch economy and supplied part or all of the livelihood of a large proportion of the people of the Netherlands. The Dutch were prepared to make large concessions to Indonesian nationalism, but did not expect to grant full independence. The United States took a hand in the struggle between the Dutch and Indonesian nationalism. It directed most of its effort toward easing Dutch demands, bringing pressure on the Dutch to end hostilities with the nationalists and, through the United Nations, helping to arrange a viable peace. The story is complex, but the main outlines can quickly be covered.

Almost immediately after the defeat of the Japanese, Indonesians proclaimed (August 17, 1945) the Republic of Indonesia, with its capital at Jakarta, the city known as Batavia by the Dutch. Because the Dutch, only recently freed from German occupation, were in no position to send troops to disarm and repatriate the Japanese in the islands, the Southeast Asia Command of the United Nations, then under Lord Mountbatten, did so; and a small force of British and Indians arrived in September, 1945, to begin the process. In the near approach to anarchy which followed, various Indonesian factions fought one another, and the moderate nationalists sought to restore some kind of order. The British and Indian troops slowly extended their control, but not without much fighting, fighting which angered Indian nationalists, for it seemed to have as its purpose the restoration of colonial rule.

In December, 1945, the British made it clear to the Dutch that further help from them would be conditioned upon Dutch willingness to negotiate with the Indonesians. The United States government was troubled by domestic criticism that Lend-Lease equipment and American-trained Dutch troops were being employed against Indonesian nationalists, and it joined with the British in bringing pressure on the Dutch. Late in December the latter complied with such grace as they could command and agreed to negotiate with the Indonesian Republic.

In February, 1946, the Netherlands announced a plan which had originally been outlined over the name of Queen Wilhelmina

in 1942 for the reorganization of the Dutch empire as a commonwealth of equal partners, somewhat akin to the British Commonwealth. In May, 1946, it proposed an implementation of that plan
by recognizing the Republic of Indonesia as a unit in an Indonesian federation. As other units of the proposed federation the
Dutch were organizing what purported to be self-governing
states in parts of the archipelago not under the control of the
Republic. The Republic countered by demanding full independence. On November 15, 1946, the Dutch and the Republic
tentatively entered into the Linggadjati Agreement, the Dutch
recognizing the Republic as the *de facto* government of the islands of Java, Madura, and Sumatra, promising to turn over these
islands to it by January 1, 1949, and undertaking to set up by that
date a sovereign, federal, democratic state, the United States of
Indonesia, of which the Republic of Indonesia was to be a unit.
The United States of Indonesia would in turn be part of the
Netherlands-Indonesian Union, headed by the Dutch Crown, thus
making actual the plan set forth by the Dutch earlier in the year.
On November 30, 1946, the last of the British troops left and the
skies seemed fairly clear for an early peace.

Peace was not so easily achieved. Each side accused the other
of violating the Linggadjati Agreement, and fighting continued.
When, on March 25, 1947, the Linggadjati Agreement was formally signed it was already breaking down. The two parties differed sharply on the interpretation of some of its terms ,and the
Dutch were going ahead with actions which the Republic resented. Yet Great Britain and the United States gave *de facto* recognition to the Republic. On May 27, 1947, the Dutch sent an
ultimatum to the Republic. The latter accepted some demands
and opposed others. On June 27, to help bring accord, the United
States urged the Republic to agree to Dutch terms and said that it
was willing to consider financial aid to an interim government.
The Dutch were unyielding, and in July began full-scale military

action. Within two weeks they overran about two-thirds of the territory held by the Republic.

Then the Security Council of the United Nations stepped in. The United States and Great Britain had been trying to induce the Republic and the Dutch to come to terms and make that act unnecessary. On August 1, 1947, in response to a request from India and Australia, the Security Council issued a cease-fire order. The Dutch disregarded it. In general the colonial powers, fearing repercussions in their respective possessions, insisted that the issue was purely domestic, and that the Security Council did not have jurisdiction. Australia, India, the Philippines, and several other states leaned toward the Republic. The Soviet-Polish bloc urged the withdrawal of the forces to the positions held before the recent fighting and the appointment by the Security Council of a commission with power to arbitrate. The United States advised compromise, for it feared that to push the Netherlands too far might weaken that state and with it the American side in the "cold war" with Russia. On August 25, 1947, the Security Council passed a resolution engineered by the United States. By this a Committee of Good Offices of three members was appointed. The Netherlands chose a Belgian member, the Republic an Australian, and the Belgian and the Australian chose an American. The committee met on the U.S.S. *Renville*, a transport, in the harbor of Jakarta.

The Committee of Good Offices arranged what was called the Renville Agreement. In the main it was that of Linggadjati. Although the U.S.S.R. denounced it as perpetuating the colonial status of Indonesia, it was adopted by the Security Council by a vote of seven to nothing with the U.S.S.R., Colombia, Syria, and the Ukraine abstaining. The Committee of Good Offices continued its work, but was stalled for months and complained that the Dutch blockade was preventing the rehabilitation of the Republic. On December 19, 1948, Dutch forces seized the capital and the most important leaders of the Republic. The Committee of Good Offices held that this was a violation by the Dutch of the Renville Agreement.

The Security Council met on the very day of the Dutch move. A strong resolution was put forward by the United States and two other members calling for the cessation of hostilities and the withdrawal of forces to the respective sides of the demilitarized zones set up by the Renville Agreement. American economic aid to Indonesia under the European Recovery Program was suspended, although aid to the Netherlands itself was continued. A Russian veto killed the resolution and the abstention of the United States, Great Britain, and their supporters blocked a similar resolution offered by Russia. The United States was clearly out of patience with the Dutch and probably also feared that if it seemed to side with the perpetuation of European imperialism as against the desire of the peoples of Asia for independence it would be aiding the spread of Communism with its excoriation of colonialism. Disturbed by the unsettled conditions in Indonesia, India called a conference of Asian, African, and South Pacific nations. This met at New Delhi in January, 1949. The resolutions passed by that gathering, somewhat toned down by the influence of the United States, called for the restoration of the Republic of Indonesia, general elections for a constituent assembly, the transfer of sovereignty, and the withdrawal of Dutch troops. Spurred by this conference, the Security Council passed a new resolution (January 28, 1949), sponsored by the United States, China, Cuba, and Norway, which set forth a plan for settlement, a plan which was not acceptable to the Dutch, and substituted a United Nations Commission for the Committee of Good Offices. Late in March, 1949, Secretary of State Acheson urged on the Dutch Foreign Minister the necessity of a Dutch policy in accord with the wish of the United Nations. Criticism of the Dutch was also vigorously expressed in the United States Senate.

All this prepared the way for a round-table conference at The Hague between representatives of the Netherlands and the Republic of Indonesia and for an agreement which settled the major issues in dispute. On December 27, 1949, the Dutch formally recognized the Republic of the United States of Indonesia as a sovereign state. In 1950 the United States gave aid to the new regime, in the form of a credit of $100,000,000 from the American Export-Import Bank and several million dollars through the Economic Cooperation Administration. By the end of 1950 Indonesia had concluded an agreement with the United States covering various phases of future technical cooperation with that country, and by November, 1951, ECA had allotted $10,600,000 for economic aid to Indonesia.

Like India, Indonesia was anxious to have an independent foreign policy without obligations to either of the two great power blocs. Like India, too, but perhaps to an even greater degree, she feared the reimposition of some form of foreign control, and was therefore somewhat suspicious of American aid, especially military aid, which might imply military commitments to the United States. In February, 1952, an Indonesian cabinet resigned in protest against the Foreign Minister's action in accepting American military aid on terms which, it was charged, were derogatory to Indonesia's independent position. Although Indonesia, unlike India, signed the Japanese peace treaty, there was much domestic opposition to this step. It was necessary for the American government to move cautiously in its efforts to aid Indonesia, lest it intensify Indonesian suspicions of its supposed imperialistic intentions.

Summary

As we look back over the brief pages of this chapter we must ask how far, by the end of 1951, the United States had succeeded in its objectives in southeast Asia.

The six years were too short a time for an accurate appraisal. The full answer could not be given until, in the course of later years, movements then in progress had developed further.

As far as could be judged late in 1951, the record was one of partial frustration, but of in the main achievement. The criteria were the avowed purpose of the United States to enable these peoples to live under governments of their own choosing which would not oppress them but would enable them to advance in freedom, education, and economic well-being, and to contain Communism. Except for Indochina—and even there to a limited degree—progress had been made toward these goals. It had been slow, especially in freedom, education, and economic well-being. That was to be expected from the nature of the problem, particularly in view of Japanese exploitation, the recent emergence from World War II, and the persistence of civil strife. Nor was the United States solely or even chiefly responsible for such advance as was registered. Yet in the main the United States had aided it. That was especially the case in the largest of the areas, Indonesia. The gains might prove ephemeral. There was no assurance that the governments under which they had been made would endure or, enduring, would not in turn exploit the many in the supposed interests of the few. Thus far, however, the gains had been real, and in general the United States had not retarded them but had assisted and furthered them.

Selected Bibliography

J. F. Collins, "The United Nations and Indonesia," *International Conciliation,* March, 1950, No. 459 (New York: Carnegie Endowment for International Peace).

L. A. Mills and associates, *The New World of Southeast Asia* (Minneapolis: University of Minnesota Press, 1949).

B. Lasker, *Human Bondage in Southeast Asia* (Chapel Hill: University of North Carolina Press, 1950).

The Role of ECA in Southeast Asia, Special Report, January 15,

1951, Division of Statistics and Reports, Far East Program Division, ECA.

L. K. Rosinger and associates, *The State of Asia: A Contemporary Survey* (New York: Alfred A. Knopf, 1951).

R. P. Stebbins and the Research Staff of the Council on Foreign Relations, *The United States in World Affairs, 1950* (New York: Harper & Brothers, 1951). See also the earlier volumes in this series.

V. Thompson and R. Adloff, *Empire's End in Southeast Asia* (Headline Series, No. 78 (New York: Foreign Policy Association, Nov.–Dec., 1949).

L. S. Finkelstein, *American Policy in Southeast Asia*, rev. ed. (New York: American Institute of Pacific Relations, 1951).

VII. THE PHILIPPINES:

A CONTINUING AMERICAN

RESPONSIBILITY AND PROBLEM

MORE THAN SOUTHEAST ASIA, THE PHILIPPINES WERE a test of the success of United States policy west of the Pacific. The Philippines had been governed by the United States from 1898 until the setting up of the Commonwealth of the Philippines in 1935. Even after that step, important ties were maintained with the United States; full independence was scheduled to come in 1946. Americans sought to guide the Filipinos into the democratic way of life as they understood that word. They introduced American political institutions and representative government. They inaugurated and developed an educational system largely on the American pattern. They granted to the Filipinos a growing share in the management of the country. American missionaries came to the islands. Among them were Catholics who wished to bring renewed vitality to their church, which enrolled a large majority of the population, and Protestants who introduced their faith. American business put more capital into the islands than into any other one country in the Far East, except possibly Japan. The Philippines received a favored place inside the American tariff wall, with the result that their economy was geared to that of the United States. While providing for the eventual termination of that privilege, the legislation which gave the islands commonwealth status continued it for some years on a declining scale.

When once accorded their full independence, could the Philippines preserve it against outside aggressors, remold their economy, and operate successfully under the democratic tradition which the United States had sought to inculcate? Informed Americans were by no means agreed on the answer. Some believed that the poverty and ignorance of the masses, and the lack of experience, the corruption, and the inefficiency among the leaders would bring disaster. Others were persuaded that the American experiment would succeed. Still others suspended judgment but hoped for the best. In 1951 the answer was not clear.

World War II greatly complicated the puzzle and demonstrated that success was by no means as assured as the optimists had believed. The Japanese quickly overran the islands, in spite of heroic Filipino resistance and the memorable stand made by American forces. Guerrilla activities proved annoying to the conquerors; but, had it not been for the return of the United States in overwhelming force, the Philippines would probably have continued indefinitely under Japanese rule. Enough Filipinos were willing to collaborate to enable the Japanese to administer the country. If it proved nothing else, the experience of World War II demonstrated the inability of the Philippines to defend their independence against a determined major neighboring power.

The destruction wrought by World War II, and dissident forces set in motion during that war, were further handicaps. The damage inflicted by the Japanese invasion, the resistance to the invaders, and the American reconquest was enormous. In proportion to the wealth and size of the country it is said to have been greater than in any other country in the Far East, not excepting Japan and China. The total damage was estimated at between $800,000,000 and $8,000,000,000, affecting, it is said, about a third of the families in the country. The disintegration of morale and the deterioration of morals were also marked. Under the Japanese the standard of living, already low, declined, and inflation mounted. The Hukbalahap, originally armed guerrillas resisting the Japanese, persisted. The Huks capitalized on the wretched conditions of the peasantry under an oppressive landlord system;

tenancy had been on the increase for many years. They were infiltrated and eventually dominated by Communists, and may have received some aid from Communist China. In the postwar years they were a continual menace to stable government. Under these circumstances the successful operation of democratic institutions of an American type was extraordinarily difficult.

There were other factors which had to be taken into account. Outstanding was Filipino nationalism. As in most of the rest of Asia, a revolutionary movement was under way, with demands for full political and economic independence and for more of the good things of life for the rank and file. While only about half of the population over ten years of age was literate in any language, a great demand for education existed and mounted in the postwar years. In contrast with most of the other countries in the Far East, the pressure of population was not a major problem except in certain areas. On the eve of World War II only a third of the arable land was under cultivation. Properly managed, the soil, so it was estimated, could support about three times the existing population. However, while the standard of living was higher than in some other Far Eastern lands, the majority of the people were desperately poor, and in 1939 slightly less than half the tilled acreage was cultivated by its owners. More than half was farmed by tenants. The islands were rich in natural resources; but industry was backward, and the chief prewar exports, besides gold, were agricultural and mining products: sugar, coconut oil, abaca, copra, tobacco products, lumber and logs, desiccated coconut, canned pineapples, and iron ore. While the racial composition was prevailingly Malay, the Chinese constituted an influential element; and some of them were inclined to sympathize with the Communism which had come to power in their ancestral fatherland.

After the defeat of Japan, immediate relief was given by the Americans. For a time the United States Army fed more than a million persons daily in Manila, and sales or gifts by American soldiers helped to meet the needs of many. UNRRA appropriated $12,000,000 for the Philippines.

The United States held to the schedule which had been set up in 1934 by the Congress, and on July 4, 1946, the Philippines became formally independent. Not long before, the Congress had passed two acts, both approved on April 30, 1946, which dealt with the Philippines. One of these was the Philippine Rehabilitation Act, which sought to aid reconstruction in the islands. It set up the Philippine War Damage Commission of three members, one a Filipino, appointed by the President of the United States. Under it the Congress voted $400,000,000 for private claims and $120,000,000 to restore and improve public property and essential public services. In addition war surplus property with an estimated fair value of $100,000,000 was turned over to the Philippines. A large proportion of this aid, it must be regretfully noted, was not used wisely, for much was spent on such luxuries as automobiles which did little or nothing to rehabilitate the national economy.

The other act approved on April 30, 1946, was officially named the Philippine Trade Act, but was usually called the Bell Act, from the Congressman who introduced it. It came out of several months of debate and lobbying by special interests in the United States who feared Filipino competition, including farm groups, and by those who wished to safeguard the privilege of Americans to invest in the islands. Some exports to the United States were placed under strict quotas to prevent the anticipated competition with American products. Others were to be admitted free of duty for about eight years. Duties were then to be increased at the rate of 5 per cent a year until 1973. Thereafter full duties were to be charged. In other words, for about twenty-eight years Filipino products were to receive preferential treatment, as before the war, but on a decreasing scale to enable Filipino economy to adjust to the altered status. This was highly important, for under the earlier arrangement the bulk of Filipino exports had gone to the United States, and to place these suddenly under full tariff would entail great hardship on a people already staggering from war losses. Similarly imports to the Philippines from the United States were to be admitted free until July 3, 1954, and thereafter a rising scale of duties was to be applied to them. In addition, the Philippine peso was pegged to the American dollar.

A feature of the Bell Act which attracted little attention in the United States but aroused a storm of criticism in the Philippines required the amendment of the Philippine constitution to guarantee to future American interests equal rights with the Filipinos in the "exploitation" of the natural resources and the development of public utilities in the new republic. The word "exploitation" had a particularly unhappy sound to Filipino patriots, for it smacked of the hated imperialism. Moreover, many Filipinos, having suffered in the war, largely, so they believed, on behalf of the United States, had expected a golden era of prosperity at the end of the war through special American favor. To them the Bell Act came as a cold douche. This was foreseen by some of the better informed in the United States, and Assistant Secretary of State Clayton had fought the provisions which were most obnoxious to the Filipinos. After much bitter discussion the required amendment was placed in the constitution of the Philippines, but the anti-American resentment which was evoked did not quickly die.

Another important development in American-Philippine relations was the signing by the two governments in March, 1947, of military agreements. The first, which was to last ninety-nine years, granted the United States the use, under certain conditions, of specified army, navy, and air bases, with the right to a number of others in case of military necessity. A second provided for a United States Military Advisory Group in the Philippines and assistance in training, weapons, and the like for Filipino forces. By these measures the United States, in effect, undertook to defend the republic against attack from the outside.

The unstable fiscal situation of the devastated and recently liberated Philippines aroused concern in the United States. In 1946 a Philippine-United States Agricultural Mission made a report. In 1947 a Joint Philippine-American Finance Commission was sent to the islands to make a detailed survey. It recommended stiffer taxation and procedures of tax collecting and the establishment of a central bank which would assume responsibility for a managed monetary system, rather than a 100 per cent reserve to support the peso on the required par with the American dollar. It also suggested licensing imports to prevent wasting the then plentiful American dollars on non-essential purchases.

Economic and political conditions in the Philippines continued to trouble Americans who were interested in the young republic. In 1950 the islands were suffering from an economic recession and the near-bankruptcy of the government. The exhaustion of foreign exchange reserves seemed imminent. The Hukbalahap, clearly Communist-led and now calling itself the Philippine People's Liberation Army, sought the overthrow of the existing government. The triumph of Communism in China aided it by furthering the conviction of the inevitabilty of Communist victory.

Accordingly in 1950 another commission was sent, called the Economic Survey Mission to the Philippines, headed by Daniel W. Bell, not the sponsor of the Bell Act but a former Undersecretary of the Treasury. It made an extensive and sobering report presenting basic data on production, income, wages, investments, taxation, and the like, and recommended remedial measures. It pointed out that the country had not yet achieved full recovery from the war. Production was about 91 per cent of 1937 levels, but because in the meantime population had increased by a fourth, per capita output was badly below prewar levels. That a better record had not been made was due to failure to invest in economic development. This meant an undue dependence on the importation of consumer goods which was made possible by a wide excess of imports over exports and dependence on the margin of foreign exchange built up by American grants for relief. The pegging of the peso to the American dollar caused price levels in the Philippines to follow closely those in the United States, and the average Filipino could not afford to buy consumer goods imported from that country. The daily wage rate in Filipino industry averaged from $1.00 to $2.50, and in agriculture hundreds of thousands worked for less than 75 cents a day. Agricultural wages had dropped between 1947 and 1949. Yet a study made by the Catholic Church reported that $2,000 was the basic minimum annual income needed by a family.

As against these low wages, profits in business and agriculture had been high—a fact which meant that the rich were becoming richer and the poor were becoming poorer. The growing poverty of the masses was contrasted with a fourfold increase of the gross national income between 1938 and 1949. Moreover, in the postwar years government budgets were more and more unbalanced. The deficit was met with a grant of $60,000,000 by the United States Reconstruction Finance Corporation, the sale of government bonds, and other borrowing. The tax burden fell most heavily on those least able to pay. As aid from the United States for rehabilitation declined, the financial embarrassment of the country increased.

The Bell Mission thought the situation grave but not hopeless and made concrete suggestions. It held that the system of land tenure was central in the economy of the country and noted that the peasant cultivator was between two millstones—the exactions of the landlord, often excessive, and the low productivity of the land. It offered specific recommendations for improvement, including amendment and enforcement of the agricultural laws so that the tenant might receive a more equitable share of the crop, better rural credit facilities, and technical and experimental work on diversification and improvement of production. It suggested increased domestic production of goods formerly imported. It recommended that a group of three American labor unionists advise in the organization of unions which should be free both from Communist infiltration and from government domination. It proposed a higher minimum wage, measures for improving public health, and a more active participation by the government in stimulating the economic development of the country.

The Bell Mission was critical of some of the features of the Philippine Trade Act of 1946 and recommended the appointment of a joint commission to study modifications of that measure. It also proposed the negotiation of a treaty of friendship, commerce, and navigation which, among other features, would "provide equitable conditions for investments."

The central task of the Bell Mission was not to analyze the current situation in the Philippines, or to recommend internal policies for that country, although these inevitably came within its purview, but to determine the most useful and effective method of American aid. Here the mission was convinced that outright grants to the Philippine government, like earlier gifts, would run the risk of dissipation, and might aggravate rather than solve the problems they were designed to meet. On the other hand, to require as a condition of aid close supervision of its expenditure and needed political changes would be criticized as interference with Philippine sovereignty. Another possibility was to withhold assistance until recommended reforms were effected. However, some immediate aid was deemed urgent. The Bell Mission chose the alternative of supervision, and recommended:

"That the United States Government provide financial assistance of $250 million through loans and grants, to help in carrying out a five-year program of economic development and technical assistance; that this aid be strictly conditioned on steps being taken by the Philippine Government to carry out the recommendations outlined above, including the immediate enactment of tax legislation and other urgent reforms; that the expenditure of United States funds under this recommendation, including pesos derived from United States loans and grants, be subject to continued supervision and control of the Technical Mission; that the use of funds provided by the Philippine Government for economic and social development be co-ordinated with the expenditure of the United States funds made available for this purpose; and that an agreement be made for the final settlement of outstanding financial claims between the United States and the Philippines, including funding of the Reconstruction Finance Corporation loan of $60 million."

In general, the report of the Bell Mission was favorably received in the Philippines. However, as was to be expected, there was some adverse criticism. The frank publicity given to objectionable conditions was resented, and opposition was voiced to the supervision proposed in connection with the suggested aid. Some government advisory groups rejected the Bell proposals on the ground that they "would constitute an infringement of sovereignty."

The situation was critical, and when William C. Foster, ECA administrator, visited Manila in November, 1950, he entered into an agreement with President Quirino which called for legislation by the Philippine Congress greatly to increase the tax load by January 1, 1951, to fix a minimum wage for agricultural laborers, and to accelerate social reform and economic development. In return the representatives of the United States agreed that their government would send a technical aid mission, particularly to assist in taxation, revenue collection, social legislation, and measures for economic development, and would join with the Philippine government in reexamining the trade agreement.

In 1951 it was not clear whether the Bell report would be fully carried out. Nor was it certain that the disaster threatening the Philippine economy and government would be averted if it were. It had been easy to slide along under the war damage grants and the sales of surplus war stocks; and no little courage would be required to brave the wrath of special interests and make the necessary changes. The basic evils of landlordism and poverty which the Hukbalahap was promising to remedy were not adequately met by the existing regime. Yet all was not dark. Much initiative had been shown in reconstruction. The sense of national solidarity was furthered by the general use of English among the educated and by a network of air routes which bound the islands together by speedy transportation. In 1951, through the impetus given by the Bell report and the Quirino-Foster agreement, taxes were drastically increased to help bring the budget into balance and a minimum wage equal to $1.25 a day was enacted for agricultural laborers. Vigorous measures somewhat reduced the Hukbalahap menace. The increase in exports due to the war in Korea helped the Philippine economy.

The Philippine adventure of the United States was not an unqualified success. Neither was it a palpable failure. The islands could not have remained in the semiseclusion and the somewhat placid somnolence which had been theirs under Spain. Inevitably they would have been drawn into the main currents of the revolutionary Far East and into world politics. Through the United States they had at least been set on the road toward independence. While officially complete, that independence was, as we have seen, still compromised by economic and military ties to the United States. On the credit side of the balance sheet of American accomplishments were the extensive educational system, the development in sanitation and public health facilities, better roads, and the building up of the economy, especially the exports. On the debit side, more of things omitted than of things done, were the lack of adequate city planning and the failure to deal with the fundamental land problem. Whether the progress so far achieved would be continued or wrecked would depend partly on the Filipinos, partly on the United States, and partly, probably very largely, upon conditions in the world at large.

Selected Bibliography

S. Jenkins, "Great Expectations in the Philippines," *Far Eastern Survey*, Vol. XVI, No. 15 (Aug. 13, 1947).

S. Jenkins, *United States Economic Policy Towards the Philippine Republic*. (New York: American Institute of Pacific Relations, 1947, mimeographed).

S. Jenkins, "Philippine White Paper," *Far Eastern Survey*, Vol. XX, No. 1 (Jan. 10, 1951). A summary, with comments, of the report of the Bell Mission.

L. A. Mills and associates, *The New World of Southeast Asia* (Minneapolis: University of Minnesota Press, 1949).

A. Ravenholt, "The Philippines: Where Did We Fail?" *Foreign Affairs*, Vol. XXIX, pp. 406-416 (Apr., 1951).

Report to the President of the United States by the Economic Survey Mission to the Philippines (Washington, D.C., Oct., 1950). The official report of the Bell Mission.

L. K. Rosinger, "The Philippines—Problems of Independence," *Foreign Policy Reports*, Vol. XXIV, No. 8 (Sept. 1, 1948).

L. K. Rosinger and associates, *The State of Asia: A Contemporary Survey* (New York: Alfred A. Knopf, 1951).

VIII. CHINA:

THE GREAT AMERICAN DEFEAT

IT WAS ON CHINA THAT AMERICAN INTEREST IN THE Far East had chiefly been centered. It was in China that after 1945 the United States experienced the greatest defeat in its history. Why that defeat? Could it have been avoided? If so, how? Could it be retrieved? If so, by what measures? Here are subjects on which much ink has been spilled and millions of words uttered over the air. We cannot hope to give the definitive analysis or the infallible answers. Yet we must not dodge the issues. Even in as brief an essay as this, we must face them and venture upon a summary and tentative conclusions.

From what we said in an earlier chapter it must be clear that, traditionally, American interest in the Far East has been directed mainly toward China. Here lives a fifth or a fourth of the human race. Here, it was believed, is the largest potential undeveloped market on the face of the earth. The dream of that market had lured merchant princes since the days of John Jacob Astor, railway builders since the Northern Pacific was projected, and statesmen from the first half of the nineteenth century. Leonard Wood, one of the greatest of American proconsuls, as Governor General of the Philippines said on at least one occasion that it was to secure entrée to the China market that the United States must retain its hold in those islands. It was ostensibly to ensure equal opportunity for Americans with nationals of other countries in the markets and the development of the resources of China that the Open Door policy was formulated and pursued.

For other and quite altruistic motives Americans were attracted to China. It had been as much from the unselfish desire to see that the Chinese, floundering in a great revolution, had opportunity to develop their own government in their own way and to preserve intact their territorial heritage as from a wish to share in China's trade and economic development that the Open Door had been a major concern in American foreign policy. Indeed, altruism may have been more of a motive than selfish interest. To aid the Chinese in their great transition tens of thousands of Americans had gone to China as Christian missionaries. More Americans had labored as missionaries in China than in any other one country. They had had a leading part in initiating China in Western education, modern medicine, nursing, public health, and agriculture. More Chinese had studied in American colleges and universities than in any other country in the Occident.

Moreover, it had been primarily to defend China against Japanese aggression that the United States had entered upon the road which led it to Pearl Harbor. To drive the Japanese out of China and give the Chinese an opportunity for independence, the United States had expended untold treasure and given the lives of thousands of its sons. It was through that effort to help China that the United States had been saddled with the unwelcome responsibility of the occupation and remaking of Japan and the occupation of South Korea; and to that the United States owed its costly involvement in the Korean war which broke out in 1950.

Yet, in spite and in part because of these efforts and sacrifices, after the defeat of Japan the United States suffered what proved to be the major reverse in all the history of its dealings with foreign nations. A government more sinister for the future welfare of China and of American interests, selfish and unselfish, in that country than one controlled by the Japanese swept Americans out of the land, and through all the techniques known to modern propaganda sought to persuade the Chinese people that Americans and the United States were and all along had been their chief enemy.

The American Record in the Far East, 1945–1951

How did this come about? Who was responsible? What was the outlook for the future? Properly to answer these questions, historical perspective is required.

First of all, we must recognize the fact that the Communist victory and the American defeat were only one stage in a prolonged and profound revolution which had been sweeping across China. That revolution began at least as far back as the 1890's and is said by some to have had its first manifestations in the Taiping movement of the 1850's and 1860's. It was due to the impact of the Occident, which brought changes to every country in Asia. In none of them, with the possible exception of Russia, where Communism and industrialization, coming from the West, produced a world-shaking transformation, was the revolution on so gigantic a scale as in China.

Why the revolution in China was more disintegrating than in such other highly civilized countries as India and Japan we must not stop to discuss at any length, although the answer may have important bearings upon the future of Communism in that land. One important factor was the rapid decline of Confucianism. For more than two thousand years the chief ideological force which shaped China was Confucianism. China was ruled by a state which was built on Confucian principles. Those principles were inculcated through an educational system which gave them chief place, and through which the leadership of the nation was trained. In the early part of the twentieth century the revolution swept out the two pillars of Confucianism—the type of education which made Confucianism central, and the Confucian monarchy. When these went, Confucianism was fatally weakened. Although many of the basic convictions and attitudes nourished by it continued, its decline left a large proportion of the younger generation adrift, with no strong moral foundation and without a generally accepted understanding of the universe and of life on which to build.

For a minority Christianity filled the vacuum. For many nationalism, heightened by contact with the West, was a partial substitute. However, it was a nationalism without a strong unifying center. Democracy as understood in the United States and Great Britain was accepted by some; but at best, by its nature, for the majority it would come, if at all, through slow growth and long experience. Communism entered, propagated by a convinced minority. While the majority were as yet unconvinced, Communism set in motion processes of mass conversion and education. Some observers believed that it could not succeed, and that eventually the majority of Chinese would reject it. That, however, was prophecy, and prophecy is notoriously fallible. To many it seemed probable that Communists would be in control in China for many years to come, perhaps for a generation or more. What China would be if it were under their tutelage for that length of time no one was wise enough to foresee. That Communism was a stage in the revolution in China seemed clear. How long that stage would last, and what would succeed it, no one could know.

A second fact which we must recognize out of the past is that for more than a century China had been weak as against foreign powers, which have encroached again and again upon what is usually considered national sovereignty. First in the 1840's and 1850's came the cession of Hong Kong to Great Britain and large territories north of the Amur and east of the Ussuri to Russia, and what the Chinese were later to call the "unequal treaties," with extraterritorial privileges to foreigners and the surrender by China of her right to fix her tariffs by unilateral action. A series of further restrictions followed, among them the development of "concessions"—one being the famous International Settlement in Shanghai, the main port of China—which were in large part removed from the operation of her administration and laws, the collection of her maritime customs under foreign supervision, "spheres of influence," the compulsory granting of leaseholds to several of the powers, and the loss of Formosa to Japan.

Then, in 1901, as the result of the Boxer outbreak, China became in effect an occupied country, with the foreigners maintaining armed forces in her capital and in Tientsin to guard their legations. China was forced to pay a punitive indemnity which for those days was deemed large. In 1904–1905 Russia and Japan fought largely on Chinese soil while China stood by, helpless. World War I was accompanied by Japanese demands, some of them granted under duress, which gave to China's island neighbor additional privileges on her soil. In the 1920's came the first incursion of Communism, at its inception fostered by Russia.

Far-reaching Japanese encroachments came in the 1930's and were succeeded by the wholesale Japanese invasion of China. At first the United States supported China's cause only with words, while continuing to sell materials of war to Japan. Then gradually American resistance stiffened, until at last America was plunged into war as China's ally. The war years brought the presence of thousands of American troops in many parts of China, the humiliating dependence of China upon American military and financial assistance, and attempts by Americans, some of them far from tactful, to control certain phases of China's policy and to mediate in China's internal dissensions. Latest of all was what, to Chinese who were not blinded by Communist convictions and propaganda, was the most extensive and sinister invasion of all, domination by Russian Communism.

Suffering from weaknesses that went back far beyond the past two centuries and from the destruction of her old values and institutions, China was unable successfully to defend herself. Because of the vast revolution which had been sweeping across the land, the Chinese were confronted with the urgent necessity of building afresh a culture and a set of institutions, inevitably a long and painful process for so large a group of mankind. But they were not permitted to do it unhindered. Their neighbors stepped in, partly, in the case of some of them chiefly, out of self-interest, but also partly out of a genuine if blundering desire to be of help.

A third fact prominent in the past century or more of China's history was the combination of foreign invasion with exhausting civil strife. Much of this had grown out of the impact of the West, and the two were, therefore, closely related, especially if foreign invasion be taken to include not only military and political operations, but also foreign trade and the incursion of Western ideas and culture. In the 1850's and 1860's the Taiping rebellion, in part the fruit of ideas from the West, laid waste some of the most fertile and populous sections of China. Beginning with 1911, China had suffered from uninterrupted civil war. Sometimes it nearly died down. At others it swelled to major proportions. China's economy and what should have been her normal life were tragically and chronically disrupted. To the civil strife foreign military invasions were added. Often China had to face both at the same time

Other factors out of the past were mounting resentment among Chinese at the compromise of their political, territorial, economic, and cultural independence, a great war-weariness, and a passionate longing for peace. The desire for independence showed itself in a wide variety of ways. The Chinese are a proud people. Until the twentieth century they were accustomed to thinking of themselves as models, the center of civilized mankind, and to having their culture copied by their neighbors. To that pride the prolonged foreign invasion was a bitter experience. The Chinese sought to emancipate themselves. For nearly two decades after World War I they seemed to be making progress. Features of the "unequal treaties" were going. Even in the 1940's, when Japan was tightening her noose about China, some gains were made. In 1943 Great Britain and the United States relinquished their extraterritorial privileges, and the United States rescinded the exclusion acts, long a source of offense to China, and permitted Chinese to be naturalized. Yet during the war there were more American troops on Chinese soil than ever before, even though they came to liberate China from the Japanese. The Chinese hoped, almost desperately, that the defeat of Japan would mean the full unification of their country—including Manchuria, so long alienated from it—under one Chinese rule and the achievement of domestic peace. In this they were bitterly disappointed. To that disappointment the Yalta agreement, to which the United States was a party, contributed.

This background of intense desire for full independence, of outraged hatred of foreign aggressive "imperialism," this prolonged sense of frustration among a proud people, must be prominently borne in mind if we are to understand the Chinese attitude toward the United States and the success of Communism in mastering China. In their propaganda the Communists rang the changes on what they proclaimed as self-interested American imperialism. They played up facts which could be adduced to support the accusation. With great cleverness, one is tempted to say with demonic skill, they distorted other facts and charged Americans and the United States with motives exactly the reverse of those from which Americans believed that they were operating. Communists also attempted to convince the Chinese, especially the youth, that a better day was at hand in which civil strife would cease and peace and prosperity would reign.

The next statement is debatable, and many well informed Americans and Chinese will disagree with it. At the time of the surrender of Japan, in August, 1945, the chances were that the existing government of China, controlled by the Kuomintang, or Nationalist Party, and led by Chiang Kai-shek, would give way and be followed by Communist domination. At the time this was by no means clear, even to the most astute observers in the United

States. Yet as we look back from the vantage point of later years we can see features in the situation, weaknesses in the Kuomintang and in Chiang Kai-shek, together with characteristics of the Communists, which give at least some ground for this opinion. The Nationalist Government had borne the main brunt of a long and exhausting war. While technically among the victors in World War II, in reality it was a defeated power. Its seeming victory had been due partly to its prolonged resistance but in the end to foreign, chiefly American, aid. It was suffering from internal divisions, from an inflation which had already reached astronomical proportions, and from considerable corruption—although not as much as some pessimists declared. Chiang Kai-shek had done an amazing job in giving the nation a degree of unity and in nerving it to resistance against Japan; but he had limitations which prevented him from meeting the almost superhuman demands made on his government first by the prolonged war and then by the defeat of Japan.

The Nationalist Government was faced by the Communists. The two had been at odds since 1927. Much of the time there had been open warfare. In late 1936 and early 1937 an ostensible peace, really only a truce, had been patched up, although probably not by written agreement, that a common front might be presented against Japanese ambitions. In theory there were two political parties. Actually there were rival governments which could not be successfully amalgamated. The Kuomintang was committed by the program of its creator, Sun Yat-sen, eventually to share its power with other parties; but its theory of government through more than one party differed basically from that of the Communists. Long accustomed to control, and, with the exception of the Communists, confronted only by minor parties, none of them strong, its leaders expected to remain dominant. The Communists had quite different convictions about the state and society. While, as a matter of tactics, they might cooperate for a time with other parties, it would be only as a means to obtaining full control. Moreover, because of the long conflict, they nourished an implacable hatred for Chiang Kai-shek and most of the leadership of the Kuomintang. The two parties could not be brought permanently into cooperation, nor would one peaceably submit to having the government run by the other as would rival parties in such countries as the United States and Great Britain.

Handicapped in this fashion, after V-J Day the Nationalist Government was confronted with the necessity of rapidly extending its administration over the areas which had been occupied by the Japanese. The Japanese army in China must be disarmed and repatriated. Over some Chinese territory, notably Manchuria, the Nationalist Government had never really exercised authority. Although it claimed legal jurisdiction over Manchuria as part of China, actually its officials and its troops were aliens in that region and would meet with the suspicion usual among the inhabitants of one section of a country for those of another section. Even in areas which had been under its administration before the Japanese invasion, including those in what had once been its stronghold, the lower part of the Yangtze valley, the Nationalist Government returned from its exile in its wartime capital, Chungking, as something of a stranger. Its officials had to deal with Chinese who had remained under the Japanese. Some of these had collaborated with the invaders, but others had paid a heavy price for resistance. The Nationalist Government was faced with the necessity of winning the cooperation of this population but, as the event proved, alienated a large proportion of its most influential leadership.

In addition to these problems, the Nationalist Government had to rehabilitate the transportation system, wrecked by long years of fighting, and to deal with what proved to be a hopeless financial situation. Its budget, strained by prolonged war and the dwindling revenues, had long been out of balance, and the deficit was met by rapidly depreciating issues of paper. It now had to face the cost of supporting its armies, which could not be quickly disbanded, especially in view of the Communist menace, of extending its administration over a vast area, and of reconstruction and rehabilitation, especially of transportation. Its system of taxation could not be restored and expanded rapidly enough to close the gap between income and expenditure. Indeed, the gulf widened. The result was increasing inflation.

What of the Communists? Did they not have to meet the same problems? Why were they able to remain intact, oust the Nationalists, and take over the entire country? Several factors contributed to their success. They were much better organized than the Nationalists and much more closely integrated under a highly disciplined leadership. Not so much of their strength was dependent on one man. Mao Tse-tung had no such dominant position among them as Chiang Kai-shek in the Kuomintang. They possessed a more unified, coherent fighting ideology than the Kuomintang. The program of Sun Yat-sen, to which the latter was officially committed, did not have the bite and drive of Communism. The Communists had not borne so much of the brunt of the Japanese invasion. Although they had operated an amazingly skillful guerrilla resistance, they had not fought so many pitched battles as the Nationalist armies. Nor had they carried on resistance over so wide a front. Their armies were much better fed and disciplined than those of the Nationalists and had more stomach for fighting, and their administration had in it very much less of corruption. They were not under the necessity of disarming and repatriating the Japanese, nor did they aim to occupy at once all of the country evacuated by the Japanese, as did the Nationalists. While they demanded, as it proved successfully, that some of the Japanese-occupied territory be theirs, they did not try immediately to move into as large an area as did the Nationalists.

Moreover, they were strongest in the north, the area in which the Nationalists were traditionally weakest. They could afford to wait until the Nationalists had been proved to be incompetent and then present themselves as the only possible alternative if the country was to be pulled out of the morass. When once the Nationalists had failed, as they did by the end of 1948, especially after the calamitous miscarriage of the effort to improve the currency in the summer of 1948 by putting paper money on a metal basis, the Communists easily walked in. The Nationalists had completely forfeited the confidence of the people, and the Communists were the only alternative to chaos.

Had the United States, by its policies before August, 1945, fatally handicapped the Nationalist Government? If different policies had been pursued, would the Nationalists have succeeded? That mistakes were made is certain. The appointment of General Stilwell seems to have been one, especially in view of his contempt and distrust for Chiang Kai-shek. Friction between the two men was a handicap to the Allied cause and probably weakened Chiang's government. Some American officials regarded the Chinese Communists as agrarian reformers rather than Communists of the Russian kind, sought to effect a reconciliation between them and the Nationalists, and believed that aid to them would assist substantially in the defeat of Japan.

Most serious of all, in the judgment of many, was the Yalta agreement of February, 1945, in which the United States consented to the reentry of Russia into Manchuria and the restoration to her of many of the privileges she had enjoyed there before her defeat by Japan in 1904–1905. This has seemed to many to have been a betrayal of China, buying Russia's entry into the war with something that did not belong to the United States, in spite of the fact that China accepted the arrangement and confirmed it in her treaty with Russia of August 14, 1945. At that time Russia promised to give military aid and moral support only to the Nationalist Government, to withdraw her troops from Manchuria (except the garrisons in the Liaotung Peninsula) within three months after the formal surrender of Japan, to keep her hands off China's internal affairs, and to avoid interference in Sinkiang.

It is said that Yalta was a denial of the high moral principles on which the United States had ostensibly fought the war, and that from the military standpoint it was quite unnecessary to bring Russia into the Far Eastern war since Japan was already defeated in 1945 and would soon have surrendered, even had Russia kept out. It is also pointed out that, let into Manchuria by the Yalta agreement, the Russians carried away much of the machinery which might have proved helpful to China in her recovery, that when they evacuated the region they left behind Japanese military equipment which was of great assistance to the Communists in their successful struggle with the Nationalists to control the region, and that they further handicapped the Nationalists in not permitting them to use Dairen, the best port in Manchuria, to send forces into the area.

We cannot certainly know whether, had these various actions by the United States not been taken, the scale would have tipped in favor of the Nationalists. The answer hinges on the weight that is given to other factors. Friction between Americans, especially Stilwell, and the Nationalists undoubtedly weakened the latter, but probably not enough to make the difference between the survival and failure of their government. The appraisal of the Communists as agrarian reformers was mistaken, and the efforts to bring them and the Nationalists together were foredoomed, as many Americans knew and said at the time. However, it is highly doubtful whether that appraisal greatly strengthened the Communists. Moreover, if the Americans had encouraged or assisted the Nationalists in an attempt to subdue the Communists while the war with Japan was in progress, the Japanese would have taken the occasion to make still further advances into China, and the Nationalists would probably have been even more badly weakened without damaging the Communists enough to prevent their later victory.

Whether, had there been no Yalta agreement, the Russians would have remained at peace with Japan is by no means certain. Indeed, it seems probable that they would have made some occasion for entering the war with her at a convenient date, so that they might have a voice in all aspects of the postwar settlement. Nor is it clear how they could have been kept out of Manchuria. Although President Roosevelt was inclined to grant their requests because of a conviction that Russia was entitled to an ice-free port in that region, it is well known that the Russians had been determined to reinstate themselves in Manchuria. They might well have found an occasion to do so, perhaps by demands on the Nationalist Government.

Even had the Russians kept completely out of Manchuria, it is not proved that the Nationalists could have established themselves in the region and excluded the Communists. In their reoccupation of east China, as in the earlier stages of their administration of Formosa, they proved singularly inept, or worse, and alienated the masses. That they would have had a similar record in Manchuria is highly probable. Indeed, there were beginnings of such a record before the Communists took over. The Communists possessed the advantage of having their centers nearer Manchuria, and through tactics not unlike those which gave them the victory in other sections of China, especially in the north, they were able to take it over. The possession of Japanese arms left by the Russians undoubtedly helped them, but it is possible that they would have succeeded without those arms and without Russian aid. This, however, is highly debatable.

It can be argued that had the United States not sanctioned Russian reentry into Manchuria, as it did at Yalta, it would have been in a better position to protest the Russian action and would have had a better standing with the Chinese and with Asians in general. It is not clear that this would have been the result. However, the United States would have had a cleaner record had President Roosevelt not made the commitment at Yalta.

Another question which is not often raised is the effect on China of the direction of the primary American effort in World War II to the Western arena. Had the United States reversed that emphasis, first defeating Japan while giving such assistance in the West as could be spared from the Pacific front, would the collapse of Japan have been sufficiently accelerated to prevent the extreme exhaustion from which the Nationalist Government suffered, with its sequel of ineffective resistance to the Communists? Had the war between Russia and Germany been thus prolonged, would Russia and Communism have been so weakened that they would have proved a less grave menace to the United States, China, and the world? We cannot know. It is arguable that, in view of the difficulties presented by the vast Pacific distances, the initial lack of preparedness in the United States, and the time required to devise the tactics and construct the equipment which eventually subdued Japan, the war against Japan could not have been pushed to a conclusion much if any more rapidy than it was. What the results of such a policy would have been on the European front must be even more a matter of speculation rather than certainty.

Had the United States been prepared to use armed force in the autumn of 1931 or even in the summer of 1937, when the aggression of Japan in China began which so weakened the Nationalist Government, the latter would undoubtedly have had a much better chance of survival. Whether in that case it would have won out over the Communists and achieved stability for China under a genuinely democratic regime is a fascinating question; but it could be debated endlessly with no final agreement. The imponderables, including the repercussions in Europe, are too many to permit convincing conclusions. It is clear that public opinion in the United States would not have supported such a war, at least at the outset, and that Washington would not have undertaken it. Indeed, had it not been for the attack on Pearl Harbor, the American public would have been by no means all of one mind even in 1941 and 1942. Naval and military action to protect Malaya and Indonesia from Japanese aggression, which would presumably have been undertaken, would probably have evoked only lukewarm support.

If the odds against a Nationalist victory over the Communists were so great in August, 1945, what possibilities were open to the United States at that time, and which of them should have been chosen? One conceivable course was complete withdrawal from China, placing on the Chinese the responsibility for disarming and repatriating the Japanese, then completely demoralized, and of putting their own house in order. In view of the historic Far Eastern policy of the United States and especially of the recent gigantic efforts put forth by Americans to liberate China, that course would hardly have been adopted. In their reaction from the war and in their desire to go about their own affairs the majority of Americans might have welcomed it, as they did demobilization; but for the United States government it was not really a possibility.

A second choice would have been to go to the other extreme and give such assistance to the Nationalist regime, conditioning it upon the acceptance of American direction, as would in effect have made that government an American puppet and China a part of an American empire in the thinly disguised form of the kind of protectorate which Great Britain once had over the native states of India. That is what the Japanese attempted to establish in China through the Wang Ching-wei regime. Steps which some Americans and Chinese suggested would have tended in this direction. To have followed this course would have involved the United States more deeply in China than ever before. It would have aroused against the United States the intense nationalism which had been one of the characteristics of recent China. It would have provided ammunition for Communist anti-American propaganda, both in China and elsewhere. It would probably also have alienated much of the non-Western and especially the Asian world, highly sensitive as it was to any hint of imperialism.

A third possibility would have been to insist, conditioning any American aid upon compliance, that the Nationalist Government first consolidate itself in one portion of China, perhaps south of the Yellow River, or at most south of the Great Wall, ignoring the rest, including Manchuria, for the time being, and leaving it to local governments or to the Communists. This, it may be argued, would have presented the Nationalist Government with a manageable task. Once it had made good its rule in a limited portion of the country, it could have dealt with the north. It would not have been the first time that China had been divided under rival regimes. That had occurred more than once, and sometimes the partition had lasted for many years. There were Americans who counseled the Nationalist Government to adopt that procedure, especially for Manchuria.

However, it was too much to expect that such a program would be followed. The Nationalists and Chinese nationalism in general had all along insisted that there must be only one government, and that it must include all China, certainly all of China in which the Chinese predominated and preferably all that had been embraced in the empire when it had been ruled by the Manchus. There were even some who dreamed of occupying all the lands that had at any time accepted Chinese suzerainty, including much of Indochina and Burma. Moreover, the Nationalist Government had never acquiesced in the separation of Manchuria from the rest of China. It would scarcely consent to relinquishing, even temporarily, its purpose to extend its administration over that area.

A fourth conceivable procedure would have been to cultivate

good relations with the Communists in an attempt to woo them from a complete committal to Russia and to at least semi-friendly relations with the United States. This, too, had its advocates. The outcome of a somewhat similar course followed by Great Britain indicates that it would have failed.

A fifth possibility, and the one which, in the main, was chosen, was to permit the Chinese to run their own government, giving such assistance in finances, civilian and technical aid, advice, and military support as would be consistent with the independence of the country. This was in accord with traditional American procedure and with the Open Door policy.

We must now attempt a summary of what was actually done. In the main this will be in chronological order; but strictly to follow the time sequence would in places be confusing.

After the defeat of Japan one of the earliest actions of the United States was to aid the Nationalist Government in occupying the parts of the country which had been in the hands of the Japanese and in disarming and repatriating the Japanese troops. It was, quite naturally and properly, to Chiang Kai-shek and not to the Communists, a regime which had no legal status internationally, that this assignment was entrusted by the Supreme Command of the Allied Powers. Since the Nationalist Government was the one officially recognized by the United States and other powers, including Russia, American aid went entirely to it and not to the Communists. Loud outcries were raised by Communist sympathizers over what was alleged to be this anti-Communist discrimination. On V-J Day the United States had about 60,000 troops in China; and it deployed these in such fashion as to assist the Nationalist Government, not to fight the Communists, but to reoccupy the regions recently ruled by the Japanese. At the request of that government 50,000 American marines were landed in North China and occupied Peiping, Tientsin, the coal mines of the north, and the essential connecting railways. Americans also helped to move Chinese troops into areas which were being reoccupied. They flew some of them into Manchuria. The Communists also moved into areas evacuated by the Japanese and disarmed some of the Japanese troops, and a race ensued between them and the Nationalists.

Soon war broke out between the Nationalists and the Communists, and many—including friends of the Communists, and many others as well—demanded that the United States withdraw its troops from China. Partly in response to this demand, and partly to avoid entanglement in China's internal affairs, the United States recalled most of its troops from the country.

Early in 1946, a United States Military Advisory Group to China was authorized. It was not to exceed a thousand officers and men. Its declared purpose was "to assist and advise the Chinese Government in the development of modern armed forces for . . . the establishment of adequate control over liberated areas in China, including Manchuria, and Formosa, and for the maintenance of internal peace and security." Eventually there was organized what was known as JUSMAG, the Joint United States Military Advisory Group, with a naval division to train Chinese crews, a staff at Nanking and a training group in Tsingtao, an air advisory division, a combined services division, and a ground forces advisory division, all coordinated under a joint advisory staff. Through the ground forces advisory division four training centers were established. Because of the deteriorating military situation in China, JUSMAG was ordered removed before the end of 1948.

It must be noted that repeatedly Chinese military authorities disregarded the advice of the Americans. The latter, out of principle not seeking to dominate, had to stand by and see courses followed which they knew would lead to disaster.

In addition to the assistance given in ways we have just described, the United States accorded military aid to China after

V-J Day in the form of supplies, naval vessels, and air equipment valued at well over a billion dollars. More than half of this was through Lend-Lease; $125,000,000 was through the China Aid Act of 1948; some was through the sale at a nominal sum of surplus military equipment, and some was through the transfer of navy vessels.

Before the end of 1945 the strife between the Nationalist Government and the Communists began giving the United States grave concern. It was clear that China needed nothing so much as internal peace. Years of foreign invasion and civil war had left her impoverished and crippled. It was obviously to the interest of the United Nations, of the United States, which had borne the main burden of foreign aid to China, and above all of the Chinese people themselves, that a long period of peace be achieved. It was the hope of the United States government that this could be obtained through negotiations. To that end President Truman sent to China one of America's most experienced and competent statesmen, General George C. Marshall, as his personal representative with the rank of Ambassador, in order to exert the influence of the United States for the "unification of China by peaceful, democratic methods" as soon as possible and for the ending of hostilities, especially in North China. Here was direct participation in China's internal affairs. As a reason for such a step it was said that a China torn by civil strife was not a proper place for American economic assistance in the form of credits or technical skills or for American military aid.

Some observers believed from the very outset that General Marshall had an impossible assignment, and that his mission was foredoomed. Certainly the odds were heavily against him. The distrust of the Kuomintang and the Communists for each other was so great, the personal enmities between the leadership so marked, and the basic political and economic theories so far apart that continuing peaceful cooperation in one government was highly unlikely.

Yet General Marshall made an honest and resolute attempt, and for a time appeared to be succeeding. In January, 1946, only a short time after he reached China, a committee of three convened, composed of himself as chairman, a representative of the Nationalist Government, and a representative of the Communists. Within three days of its formal meeting it had agreed upon a cessation of hostilities. Except that the troops of the Nationalist Government were to be permitted to continue to move into Manchuria to restore Chinese sovereignty in that area, both Chiang Kai-shek and Mao Tse-tung promised to send out a cease-fire order to their respective forces, effective on January 13. To supervise carrying out the order an Executive Headquarters was set up in Peiping made up of three commissioners, one from the Communist Party, one from the Nationalist Government, and one from the United States.

That same month, in pursuance of a plan adopted before Marshall reached China, what was called the Political Consultative Conference met at Chungking in which the Kuomintang, the Communist Party, and several other elements were represented. At the opening session Chiang Kai-shek announced it as the policy of the Nationalist Government to grant such fundamental democratic rights as freedom of speech, assembly, and association, equal legal status for all political parties, the holding of popular elections, and the release of political prisoners. After three weeks of work the Conference reached what was ostensibly unanimous accord for the reorganization of the government, the calling of a National Assembly, and, until that body should meet, the setting up of a State Council on which the Kuomintang and non-Kuomintang elements were to be equally represented. All parties were pledged to recognize the leadership of President Chiang Kai-shek. The Conference also agreed on a merger of the troops of the Nationalist Government and the Communists and on demobilization of the majority of the forces.

To see that the merger and the demobilization were effected, a military committee was appointed; and, as its executive agent, a military subcommittee was constituted composed of a representative of the Nationalist Government, a representative of the Communist Party, and, with the consent of both sides, General Marshall as adviser. On February 25, 1946, this subcommittee reached an accord for the progressive drastic reduction of both the Nationalist and the Communist armies, and the redistribution of both armies in such a way that they would be integrated into one military structure with the Communists in the minority in each region. On Marshall's strong advice, the national army thus constituted was to be purely nonpolitical; no political party was to carry on activities within it, none of its members were to engage in politics, and no party or individual was to employ it in a contest for power. The Executive Headquarters in Peiping was to be the agency for carrying through the plan.

Unhappily, these encouraging beginnings quickly met difficulties which eventually brought frustration. In the Kuomintang there were those who opposed the program, presumably because they feared the curtailment of their own power and because they distrusted the Communists. Moreover, the Communists did not wholeheartedly accept the arrangement. They, too, were critical and suspicious. Marshall suggested that the Executive Headquarters send field teams to Manchuria, where Communist-Nationalist tension was acute, to stop possible conflicts and to aid in demobilization, reorganization, and integration. The Communists were willing, perhaps because the Nationalist Government would thus recognize them in that region; but delay was experienced in obtaining permission from the latter.

In the meantime, conflict between the Nationalist Government's forces and those of the Communists was developing in Manchuria. The Russians deferred removing their troops from Manchuria. While they eventually reduced the number, they never completely evacuated the region. The delay in the partial withdrawal was partly by an arrangement between them and the Nationalist Government. The Russians loudly denounced the Americans for not recalling their troops from China. The Nationalist Government, handicapped by a lack of rolling stock and poor organization, and also by the Russian refusal to permit it to use the port of Dairen, did not move its troops into the evacuated areas at a pace equal with the Russian withdrawal. The Communists took the opportunity to step in and were aided by Japanese military supplies which, either directly or indirectly, contrary to the Russan promise in the treaty of 1945, were made available to them by the Russians. The Nationalists were angered by what they declared was a violation of the cease-fire agreement of January by which they were permitted to send their troops into Manchuria. In general the Communists were strong in the rural districts, and the Nationalist Government in the main cities and along the railways.

General Marshall attempted to effect a reconciliation and to promote peace. He directed much of his attention to Manchuria, but the situation was deteriorating also in other parts of China. He called the attention of the Nationalist Government to what he believed to be violation of the cease-fire by some of its commanders and of anti-Communist actions which needlessly heightened Communist suspicions. In June, 1946, he succeeded in bringing both sides to assent to a truce. During the truce, negotiations went on, both over Manchuria and over Shantung, for severe fighting had broken out in that province. It was in North China that the Communists were especially strong, and it was here that conflicts were fairly certain to arise when the Nationalist Government attempted to take over after the defeat of Japan.

Both Nationalists and Communists were critical of Marshall

and the United States. Many among the Nationalists, especially what may be called the right-wing elements, resented what they held to be American favoritism toward the Communists. The Communists denounced even more strongly what they claimed was undue American assistance to the Nationalists and anti-Communist discrimination. They complained of the aid to the Nationalists in military equipment and of what they alleged to be a disproportionate allocation of UNRRA relief to areas under the Nationalists. They also objected to the presence of American forces in China. While they recognized the integrity of Marshall and his desire to bring about an accord in China, they were conditioned by their doctrinaire Marxism to regard the United States as a designing, imperialist power, and Marshall as the tool, or perhaps the dupe, of that imperialism.

On the recommendation of General Marshall, in July, 1946, J. Leighton Stuart was appointed American Ambassador to China. Dr. Stuart was a missionary educator who had been born and reared in China, knew the country intimately, and had many friends among Nationalists, Communists, and those who belonged to neither camp. A man of charm, tact, wisdom, and unquestionable integrity, a lifelong friend of the Chinese who had been kept in house confinement by the Japanese during their occupation of Peiping because of his known hostility to their regime, he came to the post with unique experience and equipment.

Both Marshall and Stuart labored to bring about a cessation of hostilities. In a joint statement on August 10, 1946, they called attention to the gravity of the economic situation, which continued to deteriorate, and to the practically unanimous desire of the people for peace, and pointed out the chief areas of disagreement between the Communists and the Nationalist Government. That same day a personal message from President Truman to President Chiang Kai-shek expressed the grave concern of the American people over the worsening situation in China, saying that an increasing school of thought demanded a reexamination of American policy toward China, stating the belief that the hopes of the people of China were being thwarted by militarists and a small group of political reactionaries, and noting regretfully the trend in China to suppress liberal views.

President Chiang's reply placed the onus for the situation upon the Communists and said that the policy of the Chinese government was speedily to broaden its basis so as to include all parties and nonpartisans. In turn, President Truman expressed gratification over the efforts to settle the civil strife and broadly hinted that if civil strife were ended in China the United States would plan to assist the country "in its industrial economy and the rehabilitation of its agrarian reforms."

The relations between the Nationalist Government and the Communists went from bad to worse. Attempts of Marshall to bring the two parties to agreement failed, and the Nationalist Government angered the Communists by pushing its forces into what they considered to be their territory. They were especially roused by the Nationalist advance against the strategic city of Kalgan. General Marshall believed the move on Kalgan to be unnecessarily provocative and recommended that his mission as mediator be terminated. Alarmed by this suggestion, President Chiang agreed to a truce in the drive toward Kalgan to permit negotiations; but the Communists demanded, instead, a complete cessation of the attack on Kalgan. Part of their reluctance came from the fear that they would not have as much voice as they wished in the reorganized government.

Basic to the frustration of the United States was the fact that China was not ready for the kind of democracy which Americans knew, and in which they believed. On the surface there seemed to be two major parties in China, as in the United States. However, while ostensibly Chiang Kai-shek was prepared to work toward democracy as the Americans understood the term, he was very much a dictator in practice and would not willingly brook opposition. Moreover, the record of the Communists in China and elsewhere made it clear that their definition of democracy was utterly different from that of Americans, that they would insist on controlling any government which they entered, and that they would tolerate other parties merely as a temporary expedient. From their standpoint, multi-party or two-party government was not democracy. Then, too, the Kuomintang had been so long in the saddle that its leaders would find it difficult to work with other parties. It was split into many factions; but these were not parties in the American or British sense. Only the Communist party was strong enough to compete with it; there was no other party which could be an effective makeweight between the two. Nor could workable though unstable combinations of parties be developed as in France. Both experience and machinery were lacking for democratic government in the Western sense. Neither could be acquired quickly, particularly by a people as numerous as the Chinese and pressed by so many urgent problems of livelihood and civil strife. Time was needed, and much of it; but time was quickly running out.

In the National Assembly which met in Nanking in November, 1946, to adopt a new constitution in which a multi-party government might come into being, the Communists were, by their own decision, not present. Their absence was ominous.

Marshall and Stuart did not at once give up. During the autumn of 1946 they continued negotiations with Chiang Kai-shek and the Communists. However, the distrust of the military in the Kuomintang for the Communists mounted, Nationalist successes in the north made for confidence, and the Communist distrust of the Nationalists and the Americans grew. Marshall warned Chiang Kai-shek, rightly as it proved, that the Communists were too strong a military force to be suppressed. He felt that the only practicable solution was to bring them into the government.

Chiang held that the Communists, under Russian direction, were intent on destroying the Nationalist Government; and he was clearly right. Marshall's plan would not work. In this contradiction was much of the tragedy. The Nationalist Government was shot through and through with divisions and corruption and was too weak to eliminate the Communists by military force or police action. Yet, if incorporated in that government, the Communists would destroy it and substitute one of their own.

Marshall's usefulness as a mediator was over. He remained for a time, hoping that he might have some influence in encouraging China to adopt what from the American standpoint would be a genuinely democratic constitution. In January, 1947, he returned to the United States, his mission clearly at an end. Before leaving he issued a frank statement placing the blame on the Communists and the reactionaries in the Kuomintang and saying that "the salvation of the situation, as I see it, would be the assumption of leadership by the liberals in the Government and in the minority parties, a splendid group of men, but who as yet lack the political power to exercise a controlling influence. Successful action on their part under the leadership of Generalissimo Chiang Kai-shek would, I believe, lead to unity through good government."

Early in 1947 the United States withdrew the American personnel from the Executive Headquarters which had been set up so hopefully to implement peace. It also ordered all American marines out of North China except a small guard at Tsingtao in connection with the naval group engaged in training Chinese naval personnel.

It has been repeatedly said that, even though unintentionally, the efforts of Marshall and the cease-fire arranged by him worked in favor of the Communists—that the Nationalists had been winning battle after battle, and that the Communists took advantage of the breathing space to consolidate their forces and to prepare for what for the first time became positional warfare against the Nationalists. The implication is that, but for the cease-fire, the Nationalists would have won. It is probable that those who make this assertion are at least right in saying that the cease-fire assisted the Communists. It seems doubtful, however, whether it was responsible for the ultimate Communist victory. The basic weaknesses of the Nationalists and the elements of strength possessed by the Communists were of such a nature that the cease-fire probably at most could only hasten the Communist victory.

Yet the United States did not cease its effort through diplomacy to bring peace in China. Out of his long experience and many friendships with the Chinese, Ambassador Stuart sought to suggest reforms and ways to peace. At the request of Chiang Kai-shek he acted as intermediary between the Nationalist Government and the Communists, seeking to bring a cessation of hostilities and negotiation.

In Washington as Secretary of State, Marshall continued to give much thought to China. Out of suggestions which came to him, he recommended to President Truman that a special envoy be sent to China to study the situation and report. That unpromising task fell to General Albert C. Wedemeyer, who had had experience in China during World War II and was deemed especially competent. He was to study both China and Korea with the help of a staff. Although Chinese opinion was divided as to the wisdom of his mission he was officially welcomed; and he spent about a month in the country. Before leaving, Wedemeyer frankly said in public that he was discouraged to find apathy and defeatism among many Chinese, but that there were many honorable officials who, living on ridiculously low salaries, showed efficiency and devotion. He said he believed that the existing central government could win if it would remove incompetent and corrupt officials, not only from the national but more especially from the provincial and municipal structures, and if it would immediately effect drastic, far-reaching political and economic reforms. Except for the few liberals in whom Marshall had seen the hope of the country, Wedemeyer was denounced by the Chinese. The Communists would have none of him, and many in the Nationalist Government declared that he had not really understood China and had come with preconceived convictions rather than a genuine desire to find the facts.

Wedemeyer's official report was not made public until 1949, because American officials believed that its recommendations concerning Manchuria would provoke so much opposition in China that the situation would be made worse rather than better, and that the responsibilities which it proposed to place on the United Nations would prove an additional handicap to an already heavily burdened organization. Wedemeyer had proposed that immediate action be taken by the United Nations to stop the fighting in Manchuria and to prevent it from becoming a Russian satellite. He suggested that this area of contention be put under the guardianship of China, the U.S.S.R., the United States, Great Britain, and France. If one of these nations refused to share in the guardianship, China might "request the General Assembly of the United Nations to establish a Trusteeship, under the provisions of the Charter." If such action were not taken, he believed that Manchuria might be "drawn into the Soviet orbit, despite United States aid, and lost, perhaps permanently, to China." The suggestion was clearly impracticable, partly because of the initial storm of criticism which it would evoke from the Nationalist Government, the Chinese Communists, and Russia, partly because such joint guardianships seldom work unless one of the guardians, as in the occupation of Japan, is clearly dominant, and partly because the United States, on which the major load would have fallen had it been named joint guardian or trustee, would have been quite unwilling to accept. This would have meant the kind of embroilment in China which proved disastrous to Japan, and it would also have heightened the tension with Russia.

Wedemeyer also recommended that military and economic aid be accorded to China over a period of at least five years. However, it was to be given only if China requested it, and only if she also asked for American advisers in its application. If such aid produced results, further assistance could come from the Export-Import Bank, the International Bank for Reconstruction and Development, the International Monetary Fund, and private Chinese and foreign capital. All should be done in accord with the responsibilities of the United States as a member of the United Nations.

Wedemeyer was not very hopeful. He reported a situation which was rapidly deteriorating. His recommendations, while not those of despair, were obviously offered with full realization that the odds were against their adoption. They seemed to him to provide the only way in which the United States could be of effective assistance, but he evidently believed that the chances were against their being carried out.

The United States had not waited for Wedemeyer's report to send financial aid to China. Since 1937 it had been extending such assistance. It was officially reported that before V-J Day the military aid totaled $845,000,000; and that from V-J Day to March 31, 1949, the assistance, for both military and civilian purposes, had reached the vast aggregate of slightly over $2,000,000,000 in grants and credits, together with sales of surplus government property which had cost the United States slightly over $1,000,-000,000, for which China paid $232,000,000. Of these large sums $267,000,000 had come through the Economic Cooperation Administration and $46,400,000 through the United States foreign relief program. These were outright grants. Substantial credits had been authorized through the Export-Import Bank and other agencies. After V-J Day military aid through Lend-Lease amounted to nearly $700,000,000, plus naval vessels which cost the United States $141,300,000, and a grant under the China Aid Act of 1948 of $125,000,000.

As was almost inevitable in the handling of such large sums through machinery which had to be hastily devised under the urgent and disorderly conditions of the times, much of this was unwisely expended. Some of it went into equipment which was quite unadapted to Chinese needs. Some was administered by Americans who were unfamiliar with China or were in other ways incompetent. In proportion to the population of China, it was much less than what was given to the Philippines, or what went into the rehabilitation of Japan. Yet it was a very considerable sum. It was several times as much as the total pledged by China to all nations under the famed Boxer Indemnity of 1901. Even by the astronomical standards of the 1940's it was large. Much of it was spent efficiently. For example, it helped to keep alive the population of some of China's coastal cities. The Joint Commission on Rural Reconstruction, set up on October 1, 1948, was run by Chinese and American experts and gave promise of success which might have been realized but for the worsening of the position of the Nationalist Government. In its brief period of operation on the mainland, and later in Formosa, it could point to a very considerable achievement. Americans looked with a wry smile at their substantial aid to China as they contrasted it with the much smaller loan later promised to the People's Republic of China by the U.S.S.R., and as they reflected on the seemingly small returns which had come from it either in good will toward the United States or in solving China's basic problems.

We must also recall that the United States had begun in 1943 to put its relations with China on the basis of complete equality, and had ended, once for all, the "unequal treaties" which had long been a cause of complaint from sensitive Chinese. The principle of equality was prominent in a treaty of friendship, commerce, and navigation between the two countries which was signed in November, 1946.

The fears of the friends of China who had watched the deterioration of the Nationalist Government were substantiated. True, that regime did not immediately collapse. In April, 1948, the National Assembly authorized by the new constitution met in Nanking. Its chief duties were the election of a President and a Vice President. At the outset Chiang Kai-shek refused to allow his name to be put forward. Eventually he yielded to pressure, perhaps in accordance with a traditional Chinese procedure which called for such a ritual of modest reluctance, and was chosen President. In opposition to Chiang's wishes, Li Tsung-jen, once a rival war lord, was elected Vice President.

Yet the tide of battle was running against the Nationalists. The year 1946 saw the high water mark of the Nationalist reoccupation of China. They had cleared the Communists from much of the north, especially the main cities and the railways. They had made advances in Manchuria. They greatly outnumbered the Communists in men and, thanks to aid from the United States, were much better armed. However, with notable exceptions they were poorly officered and even more poorly clothed, fed, and disciplined. They were without conviction to impel them to fight. Opposed to them was an army well fed, welded into an effective fighting force by a careful indoctrination which brought conviction, and led by officers who lived as simply as the men and were fanatically committed to their cause. It was the most effective army which China had seen for many years. In discipline and determination it may never have been equaled in China, for by long Confucian tradition the soldier was looked upon with disdain.

Under these circumstances the armies of the Nationalist Government were pushed back. In 1947 they began to fail in Manchuria. In 1948 they lost the key city, Mukden. In January, 1949, the Nationalist armies in Peiping and Tientsin capitulated. In

1949 the rule of the Nationalist Government collapsed so rapidly that the Communist leaders in Peiping had difficulty in keeping in touch with their armies which were moving into the vacuum left by the Nationalist retreat. In April, 1949, the Communists took Nanking, the Nationalist capital. In May, 1949, they occupied Shanghai, China's chief port, and Hankow, the great commercial city of Central China. In October they took Canton, the main city of South China and the historic home of the Kuomintang. Soon Sinkiang and most of the northwest passed into Communist hands. The Nationalist Government transferred its headquarters to its wartime capital, Chungking, west of the Yangtze gorges, but it was soon driven out. Before the middle of 1950 it had lost all the mainland and the island of Hainan and was confined to Formosa and a few near-by islands.

On the mainland for a time numerous bands kept up a resistance to the Communists. The Nationalists hopefully claimed them, but it is probable that the majority in the bands—perhaps the overwhelming majority—had taken to banditry, in accordance with long Chinese tradition, as a means of livelihood in an age of disorder when for many it was the alternative to beggary and starvation. They were anti-Communist, but not from any desire to see the Kuomintang and Chiang Kai-shek back in power.

From the preceding pages, the reasons for the rapid collapse of the Nationalist Government must be fairly obvious. However, the reasons need to be rehearsed and summarized, because a correct appreciation of them is important in estimating what policy the United States would do well to adopt, whether toward the Nationalist remnants on Formosa or toward the regime set up in China by the Communists.

First of all, American officials repeatedly declared that the cause of the Nationalist debacle was not a lack of military supplies from the United States, and that not a single major battle was lost by the Nationalists as a result of a dearth of military equipment which the United States might have provided. Indeed, they maintained that much of the equipment which the Communists used against the Nationalists, and were later to bring to bear against the forces of the United Nations in Korea, was American in origin, abandoned by the fleeing Nationalists, taken from them, or surrendered when Nationalist units capitulated to the Communists. Some, it was admitted, was of Communist manufacture and some was former Japanese equipment, taken during the war or after V-J Day. Yet part of the defeat of the Nationalists was by arms which Americans had given them, and which they had not been strong enough to keep. This contention has been stoutly denied, and some Americans have laid the Nationalist debacle squarely to the alleged failure of the United States to give the Kuomintang armies the kind of equipment which was needed in sufficient quantity to enable them to win. The issue is real and will probably long be debated. However, the evidence seems to be on the side of those who have insisted that the cause of the Nationalist collapse was not in the failure of the United States to provide munitions.

A major reason for the Nationalist defeat was that the Kuomintang, the national government run by it, and Chiang Kai-shek had completely lost the confidence of the Chinese people. Rightly or wrongly, public opinion held the Nationalists responsible for the disasters which had overtaken China. In the days of the Confucian empire a dynasty was said to have "lost the mandate of Heaven" when it had proved incapable of averting a series of disasters, whether man-made or natural. It then collapsed before the blows of another aspirant for the throne; and the latter, if successful, was regarded as having received the mandate of Heaven until his house, in turn, proved to be chronically incompetent. Although it was now nearly forty years since the empire had gone, something of the same attitude survived. The popular mind, without perhaps using those precise words, regarded the Nationalists as having forfeited the mandate of Heaven.

That there was corruption in the Kuomintang and the government dominated by it is clear. Although Chiang Kai-shek was probably not directly involved, corruption was present on very high levels and was widespread in the lower brackets of national, provincial, and local administration. This was not new in China. One long-time foreign resident declared that there was less of it than in any Chinese government he had known. As Wedemeyer had gladly said, there were honest, hard-working, patriotic men in the Nationalist ranks; but they were too few to save the whole. We have pointed out that, in the areas the Japanese had occupied, the attitudes and actions of Kuomintang officials returning from unoccupied China had alienated thousands. They treated many local residents as though they had been traitorously collaborating with the Japanese, when they had suffered for their anti-Japanese activities. In Formosa the initial regime set up by the Nationalist Government was notorious for exploitation and corruption.

The police measures taken by the Nationalist Government to ferret out and crush critics, especially those accused of Communism, made for antagonism, especially among students and other intellectuals. Yet it failed to suppress gangsters and, in some cases, was in unholy alliance with them. The protection by officials of landlords in their exactions from their tenants, and of food hoarders and speculators in times of dearth, also made for bitterness and played directly into the hands of the Communists, who had the policy of eliminating the landlords and distributing their holdings among the peasants. The Kuomintang was torn by factions. Chiang Kai-shek was accused of favoring his friends at the expense of his enemies in the party, insisted upon retaining control, and was said to have contributed to the defeat of some of the Nationalist units by refusing support to their commanders.

The final loss of confidence was because of the failure of the

Nationalist Government to control inflation and prices. The inflation, as we have said, was due primarily to the Japanese invasion and to the lack of balance between the heightened expenses incident to resisting it and the loss of revenues from areas occupied by the Japanese. Conditions continued to become worse after V-J Day, for the government had the expense of reestablishing its administration in the regions formerly occupied, of restoring the transportation system, of supporting the swollen armies, and of carrying on the war against the Communists. The inflation seems to have been aggravated by measures deliberately taken by the Communists in their warfare against the Nationalists. To improve the situation, the Nationalist Government in the summer of 1948 issued a new currency which was supposedly supported by gold, and ordered the surrender of all gold, silver coins, and foreign currency. Thousands of Chinese loyally obeyed. Within a few weeks the new currency went the way of the old. Thus within four years Chinese who lived in areas which had been controlled by the Japanese were disheartened by the experience of having three currencies in succession become worthless—one issued by the Japanese puppet government and two by the Nationalists. Here were distress, lack of confidence, and economic disintegration, all compounded. These, added to the other causes, led almost all to say that anything, even Communist rule, was better than existing conditions.

If, in appraising the policy of the United States under the new situation in China the reasons for the defeat of the Nationalist Government must be determined, it is equally important to know the positive reasons for the success of the Communists, to strike what bookkeepers would call a trial balance of their performance in the brief period between the time when they took over the entire country and the beginning of 1952, and, in view of the effort of the United States to contain Communism, to inquire into their relations with Russia and with the world-wide Communist movement.

To all who have followed events in China, even cursorily, the reasons for the triumph of the Communists must be fairly clear. They were the one viable alternative to the Nationalists. The other parties were weak, poorly organized, and without an army. None of the few war lords surviving from an earlier stage in China's revolution was wise enough, or had a strong enough army, to make an effective bid for power on a national scale. The Communists had a tightly knit organization, led by men of fanatical convictions, which could quickly be expanded to cover the entire country. The Communist Party was carefully recruited and highly disciplined by thorough instruction in its principles and by processes of self-examination, criticism, and confession which had been developed to meet the Chinese situation. Propaganda was singularly effective in cartoons, pamphlets, slogans, songs, and folk dances. The Communists announced themselves as "liberators," and each acquisition of territory as the "liberation" of that area. Their army was well fed and well disciplined, and its treatment of the populace in the process of "liberation" was in striking and favorable contrast to that of most of the hordes that had served under the Kuomintang. Its officials were hard-working; they dressed and ate simply, almost ascetically, and were devoted to what they believed to be the welfare of the people. In this they were the exact opposite of a large proportion of the officials of the government which they displaced.

In many ways the initial achievements of what the Communists called the People's Republic of China were laudable. By the summer of 1951 the railways had been put in running order, and much of the other essential transportation had been restored. While there was still an undetermined amount of armed resistance, it was not organized on a national basis. In several cities gangsterism had been suppressed. Some of the mass executions to which critics pointed were of these elements. The advance of inflation had been curbed, and currency and prices had been fairly well stabilized. Hoarding had been made unprofitable.

In the dubious bracket must be placed progress toward the solution of the basic economic problems of the country aside from the currency. Like their predecessors, the Communists faced the problem of the livelihood of the largest mass of population on the planet. In spite of the fearful toll of war, pestilence, and famine, that population was huge and may even have been increasing. Critics declared that the Communists were starving the farmers to feed the cities and the army. They pointed to the undoubtedly burdensome taxation, much of it in the form of levies on the farmer's grain. They declared that the promise of grain to Russia and India could be fulfilled only by tightening the belts of the Chinese, possibly to the point of famine. They said that famine conditions were widespread.

The Communists insisted that there was no serious shortage of grain, that they had effected a better distribution of the existing supplies, had repaired dikes and improved irrigation, and, by impounding surpluses where they existed, had made it possible to meet dearth elsewhere. They reported that the production of cotton, on which much of the clothing of the Chinese depended, had mounted. They claimed that in Manchuria, where, thanks to the Japanese, most of the industry of the country was found, essential rehabilitation was taking place, aided by the return of equipment which the Russians had carried away when they occupied the region after the fall of Japan. The Communists also pointed to the confiscation of the estates of the landlords and their redistribution among the peasants who actually farmed them. They declared that whatever inefficiency might have been anticipated by the breaking up of the cultivated soil into minute holdings was being corrected by cooperative farms and farming operations.

The leading Communists were well aware that China could not be made over in a day, that full-scale socialism could not be put into effect immediately, and that, possibly even more than in Russia, true Communism must be postponed to the distant future. Although their propaganda held forth the prospect of the end of poverty and the achievement of plenty, they knew that this goal would not be quickly or easily attained. At the end of the year 1951 it was still uncertain whether the Communists would make continuing progress toward it, or would fail as badly as the Kuomintang. Participation in the Korean War must have put a burden on the already badly strained economy of the country, but the effect was not plain to the outside world.

From the standpoint of the kind of democracy represented by the United States, the chief items on the debit side of the balance sheet were clear in their main outlines. The Communists were pressing their system on China with no regard for the individual. To them individualism was an evil, whether that traditionally associated with China or that which they saw in the "capitalist," "imperialist" West. The regard for the welfare of the individual, with his complementary rights and responsibilities, which is basic to democracy as the United States has understood it and attempted to practice it, is alien to Communism. Communism is frankly atheistic. It not only denies the power of God and the self-giving love seen by Christians in Christ, but also scoffs at the Christian conviction of the worth of the individual as the child of God, with an eternity before him of growing fellowship with God and with other individuals in a society of the children of God. Although this conception of the infinite value of the individual is only dimly appreciated by many, it has been at the root of American democracy and of the democracy of Western Europe. Historically at least, it has been a major source of the humanism which, although doubtful of the existence of God or denying it, is potent in the liberalism of the West. This idea of

God, even the being of God, and its corollary in the possibilities in human nature were emphatically rejected by the Communists, both in China and elsewhere.

The Communists set about the mass "reeducation" of the Chinese to inculcate their views of the nature of man and of human history. They attacked what remained of Confucianism, the traditional Chinese family, and the ethics associated with Confucianism and the family. In places they set children to denouncing their parents. They also encouraged the "emancipation" of women. The Confucian heritage, already badly undermined by the disappearance of the Confucian monarchy and the old educational system, was certain to be further weakened by this fresh onslaught. Its values, undoubtedly great, would tend to be lost to the Chinese.

With their disregard for the individual and antagonism to the historic Chinese family and its ethical standards and social obligations, Chinese Communists were clearly totalitarian and were determined to regiment China and their fellow-Chinese. They aimed at what they believed to be the welfare of the whole, but the individual must either conform or be "liquidated." By the end of 1951 hundreds of thousands had been thus put out of the way. Public denunciations and mass executions mounted, especially south of the Yangtze, where the Communists had more recently come to power. Many persons thus dealt with were gangsters or in other ways had battened off their neighbors. Many, however, were innocent members of a structure which the Communists wished to sweep aside. Numbers who had supported the Nationalist Government honestly went over to the new regime, believing it to be the lesser of two evils. However, thousands of them later faced elimination as suspected handicaps to the full establishment of the new order.

How far, in all this, were the Chinese Communists tools of Russia? To what extent could they be counted on by the Kremlin in its struggle with the non-Communist world led by the United States? Here the evidence was mixed, and opinions differed.

Some facts were well established and were not seriously disputed. It was clear that the Chinese Communists were Communists, convinced adherents of the Marxist view of the universe, the nature of man, history, and the historical process, as interpreted and expounded by those now dominant in Russia. In the early days of the "liberation" pictures of Mao Tse-tung and Stalin were conspicuous and ubiquitous. The myth that the Chinese Communists were agrarian reformers and had little connection with Moscow has been exploded by the course of events.

It was also clear that Chinese Communists regarded the United States as their archenemy, and as the chief bulwark of the "capitalism" and the "imperialism" they associated with the stage of society from which they believed mankind to be moving by the inexorable course of history. They felt bound to hasten that process and to "liberate" mankind in general and China in particular from what they deemed to be the fetters of the old order represented by the United States.

The anti-American propaganda had been accelerated and heightened by the actions of the United States, first in aiding the Nationalist Government, then in preventing the "liberation" of Formosa and the admission of the People's Republic as the representative of China in the United Nations, and later in leading the resistance of the United Nations to the North Korean invasion of South Korea and to the Chinese Communist intervention in Korea. Yet antagonism to the United States had begun before V-J Day because of deeds and policies of some American representatives which were interpreted as being anti-Communist. Even without concrete instances at which to point, Communist interpretation of history would have led Chinese Communists to regard the existing order in the United States, with its wealth and power, as the outstanding menace to Communism and to what the leaders of the People's Republic were set on achieving.

What was the nature of the Chinese Communists' ties with Russia? On that, informed opinion differed. There were persons who believed that the Kremlin determined the main lines and some details of the policy of the People's Republic of China. They said that the Kremlin was too wise to do this in overt dictatorial fashion. They believed that the leaders of the U.S.S.R. had burned their fingers badly in China in the 1920's and learned from that experience to respect Chinese nationalistic sensibilities. Yet they maintained that Moscow astutely pulled the strings, and that the Chinese Communists danced, puppetlike. They pointed out the presence of growing numbers of Russian "advisers" in China, the flood of propaganda material prepared and printed in Russia and used in China, the prominence of pictures of Stalin, and the close approximation of the pattern of the Communist program in China to that in the Russian satellites in Europe. They called attention to the undoubted fact that Chinese Communist propaganda pointed to Russia as the leader in the Communist world revolution, the outstanding exponent and example of the new age which was to be ushered in by the wave of the future, and as the elder brother who, after the manner extolled in traditional Chinese ethics, was aiding the younger brother, China, in the march into that new day.

Other persons believed that the People's Republic had not been controlled by Russia, or at least not fully controlled. Some held that the Chinese Communists were also Chinese nationalists, in spite of Communist ideology which denounced nationalism and asserted that it, like the state, would wither away. Some were of the opinion that there were at least two factions in the Chinese Communist leadership, without agreeing as to what these were. It was sometimes said that there was a faction, headed by Mao Tse-tung, which stressed Chinese interests and would on occasion go against the wishes of the Kremlin. It was even suggested that

Chinese intervention in Korea in the autumn of 1950 was against the will of or at least not on the advice of Moscow. Another faction, it was often averred, including Li Li-san and Liu Shao-chi, wished to conform fully to the desires of the U.S.S.R.; this element was said to be especially strong in Manchuria. Attention was called to the quite obvious unpopularity of the Russian "advisers," to an often ill concealed dislike and contempt for them, and to the fact that a whispering campaign led to the removal of the pictures of Stalin from their customary prominence in movie theaters in at least one major city.

Between these two views of the relations with Russia it was probably unwise to choose, especially because of the confessedly incomplete evidence thus far available. Indeed, it might be unnecessary to choose. It was conceivable that the frictions which developed were merely those attendant on any real collaboration in a genuine alliance.

How long were the Communists to be in control in China? Here most experienced observers were unwilling to venture a prediction. Most of them would guess that they would be in power for at least a decade. Some would say that, unless major changes came in the world at large, such as the elimination of Communist rule in Russia (to their minds unlikely in the near future), the period would be twenty-five or fifty years. Probably a majority would agree that in 1951 there was no prospect of successful opposition to Communist rule by any Chinese force.

Opinions differed as to the popularity or lack of popularity of the Communists in China. Those familiar with China hesitated to generalize about the entire country or to do more than report their impressions of conditions at the moment in the area with which they were acquainted. In general they agreed that most of the older generation were guardedly skeptical or even hostile to the Communists, and that some were still friendly to the United States. In general they were also of the opinion that the younger generation, including especially the students, were caught up in the Communist sweep and were either enthusiastic or willing to go along with it as giving the only opportunity for a livelihood. By 1951 some of the intelligentsia were reported to be restive under the restraints on their liberty and were complaining that the level of education, already low because of the long years of revolution, civil war, and foreign invasion, was sinking. In 1951 there seemed to be a growing number who, in spite of the weaknesses of the Kuomintang and Chiang Kai-shek, would have welcomed the return of that regime.

The regime maintained by the Nationalists on Formosa, while regarded by the United States as the legitimate government of China, could not win and hold a substantial footing on the mainland, even with American backing—so most observers agreed, although a minority took quite the opposite view. It was giving the island a better administration than it had had since V-J Day; but its army had much dead wood and, even if reequipped and trained from the United States, would be of very dubious effectiveness on the mainland. Its record was against it. The Formosan remnants of the Nationalists were counting on American help and were hoping that the advent of a full-scale war between the United States and Russia would enable them to recover China. That, in the judgment of most observers, was wishful thinking.

Since no Chinese force was likely soon to unseat the Communists, presumably the only probability of their collapse was before overwhelming force from the outside, possible only from the United States, or by inner deterioration such as had been experienced by the Kuomintang, and factional dissension within the Communist Party or the army. Some observers were convinced that Communism could not persist in China. They believed that traditional Chinese individualism, family loyalty, and humor would eventually reject it. They held, too, that Communism could not solve the economic problems of China. Eventually it, too, would be adjudged to have lost the mandate of Heaven and would follow the Kuomintang into desuetude. Yet, barring events on the outside, that time seemed remote.

The question inescapably arose of what policy, under these circumstances, the United States should adopt toward China. On that there were many opinions; but the government followed a course which tended to be increasingly intransigent toward the Communist regime. The mounting denunciation of the United States by the Chinese Communists and their intervention in Korea stiffened the American attitude.

Some Americans urged that the United States equip and supervise the training of the Nationalist forces on Formosa for an invasion of the mainland. They believed that by 1951 enough Chinese had been alienated by Communist methods to rise in welcome. After the Communist intervention in Korea they advocated bombing the ports of China. Most of them disavowed any purpose of sending American troops to China. The critics of this proposed course held that, judging by its past record, the Nationalist army was undependable, had no real heart for fighting, and if sent to the mainland would soon be dissipated. While granting that a large proportion of the Chinese might be anti-Communist, they declared that by tradition the Chinese masses did not actively cooperate with any faction, and that, while their opinion might affect the result, as in the overthrow of the Kuomintang, they could not be counted on to swell the ranks of the anti-Communist armies. Moreover, so the critics said, all-out aid to the Nationalists would almost certainly be followed by the dispatch of American forces; such an invasion would divert energy from the main front against Communism, western Europe; and like the Japanese invasion it would probably bog down. If it did not bog down, but overthrew the People's Republic, the result would be chaos, and the real sufferers would be the Chinese masses; for the Kuomintang had proved itself incompetent, and there was no practical alternative to Communist rule.

On the other hand, some Americans believed that the United States must sooner or later recognize the People's Republic as the legitimate government of China. A small minority of these were sympathetic with Communism. The vast majority who favored recognition did so reluctantly; they did not like Communism but pointed out that the People's Republic was the effective government of China, that it would last many years, and that, as the United States had officially recognized the Communist regime in Russia as in fact the government of that country, so, eventually, it must give such recognition to the Communist regime in China. Moreover, so they argued, that act would prove to India and other Asian nations that the United States was willing to accept the decision of the Chinese as to what regime they would have, while refusal of recognition was evidence that the United States, in imperialist fashion, was attempting to dictate to the Chinese.

The advocates of recognition differed as to the form it should take. A few wished full cooperation, holding that this would eventually bring similar cooperation from the People's Republic and might even wean it from Russia and make it something akin to the Tito government in Yugoslavia. Critics of this policy pointed to the fact that Great Britain had already recognized the People's Republic, but the latter had not reciprocated and had demanded concessions which the British were unwilling to make. Some wished selective cooperation with the People's Republic, holding that only through that regime could the United States retain contact with the Chinese people, and that working agreements might be reached on a number of political, economic, and cultural levels, but it was pointed out on the other hand that the Chinese Communists would demand as the price of even limited cooperation the withdrawal of all American support from the Nationalists on Formosa. This would mean the Communist "liberation" of Formosa and the seating of Chinese Communists in the United Nations as the representatives of China.

Still others maintained that, without supporting a Nationalist invasion of China, the United States should keep aloof, withholding recognition of the People's Republic until it could be seen whether it would prove stable, would agree to abide by existing treaties with foreign powers, and would be a law-abiding member of the family of nations. In the meantime they would have the United States continue actively to contain Communism and, by all means short of war, discourage its further spread in eastern Asia. Moreover (so they could say), if the United States recognized the Communist regime a rush to recognize the fruits of Communist military triumph would shake the non-Communist governments in South Korea, the Philippines, and elsewhere to their foundations. Against recognition could be urged as precedent the Stimson Doctrine of 1932 by which, following still earlier precedents, the United States had denied recognition to the regime which the Japanese had set up in Manchuria, under the name of Manchukuo.

This was the course that the United States followed in the main.

The policy of the United States was beset with many difficulties. The recognition of the People's Republic by a number of governments not in the Soviet bloc, including notably Great Britain and India, threatened a break in the anti-Communist front. In the United Nations on September 27, 1949, the representative of the Nationalist Government made what in effect was a formal demand for the support of that body in its quarrel with the Communists by asking a flat condemnation of the U.S.S.R. for alleged violations of its August, 1945, treaty of friendship and alliance with China and of the charter of the United Nations, and for a recommendation to all members of the United Nations to refrain from recognizing the Chinese Communist regime. A possible threat of the People's Republic to Hong Kong posed the question of whether the United States would acquiesce in the seizure of that British colony.

The Chinese Communists early made the situation embarrassing for the United States. While professing no animosity toward the American people (some, indeed, talked of "liberating" it from its supposed Wall Street masters), they were increasingly critical of the American government. In the autumn of 1948 they confined the American consul at Mukden, Angus Ward, and his staff to his compound and kept them cut off from the outer world for six months after Washington had officially closed the post. In October, 1949, they arrested Ward and four subordinates on the charge of "assaulting" a former Chinese employee, held them incommunicado more than four weeks pending trial by a "people's court," and released them only after strong pressure, with the statement that they had been tried and found guilty and their sentences had been commuted to deportation.

In January, 1950, the United States withdrew its consular and diplomatic staff from the mainland in protest against the seizure of some of its property in Peiping. The Communists were voluble in their charges that the United States was supplying the Nationalists with the planes which were bombing the cities of China. This was in spite of the fact that on January 5, 1950, President Truman formally declared that the United States would not give military aid to the Nationalists, that it had no predatory designs on Formosa or any other Chinese territory, and that it had no desire to acquire special rights or privileges or to establish military bases on the island. In December, 1950, following the Chinese Communist intervention in Korea, the United States imposed drastic restrictions on trade with Communist China, and shortly afterward the Peiping government seized all American property in China and "froze" American bank accounts there.

Russia emphatically took the side of the People's Republic, and demanded that the Nationalists be ousted from the United Nations and the People's Republic be given its seat in that body. When, largely because of the opposition of the United States, that body did not assent, the Russian representatives walked out in January, 1950, from most of the units of the United Nations, including the Security Council, and continued to boycott them for some time.

In the domestic scene the Administration, especially the Department of State and Secretary Acheson, was loudly assailed by its critics, chiefly Republicans, for alleged softness to the Communists and was charged with allowing its China policy to be influenced by Communists or "fellow travelers."

The outbreak of war in Korea in June, 1950, led to further action by the United States. On June 27, President Truman ordered the fleet to resist any Communist attack on Formosa or the Pescadores, but also asked the Nationalists to cease their air attacks on the mainland and their blockade of the Communist-held coast of China. He said that the disposition of Formosa, taken from Japan during World War II, would await a peace treaty with that country or action by the United Nations. Presumably this was in deference to persons who believed that to permit the Communists to take over the island, as they were preparing to do, would jeopardize the defenses of the United States, and was at the same time an effort to allay the suspicion, so widely held and loudly proclaimed, that the United States was using the Nationalists as a cat's-paw in sinister designs on the Chinese people.

Moreover, the activity of the Chinese Communists in Korea which began late in 1950 seemed effectively to preclude early recognition of their regime by the United States. Recognition became especially unlikely after the branding of Communist China by the United Nations as an aggressor.

In 1951 the United States continued aid to the Nationalist Government on Formosa. It maintained diplomatic relations with it as the legal regime of China. While professing readiness to abide by the decision of the United Nations, it made clear that it did not favor the admission of the representatives of the People's Republic. In February, 1950, the Congress extended the time until June 30, 1950, for the expenditure of the remaining $104,-000,000 of the sum authorized under the China Aid Act of 1948. For the fiscal year of 1951 the residue was assigned to various uses in non-Communist China. This was largely administered under the Economic Cooperation Administration (ECA). In December, 1950, the shipment of arms to Nationalist China was resumed. In 1951 a United States Military Assistance Advisory Group was sent to Formosa to assist the Nationalist forces and to supervise the distribution of arms to be provided for them under the new policy of the resumption of arms aid to the Nationalist Government. In 1949 under the auspices of JCRR (Chinese-American Joint Commission on Rural Reconstruction) and aided financially by ECA, a comprehensive program of rural improvement was launched on the island. ECA also supplied fertilizer which contributed to a substantial increase in the rice crop.

Had the United States been as badly defeated in China as, from the perspective of 1951, it seemed to have been? That it had suffered a striking reverse was clear. The Communists, dominant on the mainland, were vociferously hostile. Most Americans, whether diplomats, businessmen, or missionaries, had left the country or were seeking to leave. Some Americans were being deported for alleged offenses against China. Churches founded and aided by Americans were being persuaded or forced to cooperate with the People's Republic and to sever all ties with fellow Christians in the West. Many Chinese trained under American auspices were working with the Communists. Many others, unreconciled, had left the country. Some had been killed as "reactionaries" or American "spies." It was clear, as it had been for many years to the discerning, that democratic institutions as Americans knew them could not soon be successfully reproduced in China. Democracy, as Americans understood it, would be at best a slow growth and—if and when it took root—would work out institutions and express itself in ways peculiar to China. That would be true in all phases of society, whether political, educational, economic, or religious.

The year 1951 was too early to reach a fair appraisal. Perhaps one could never be made. Even in later generations historians could not be sure what would have been the course of events if other policies had been followed. What, for example, would have been the outcome had the United States not been drawn into war with Japan? No one could certainly know. It seemed clear that in the realm of the spirit, where the statistically minded are inevitably baffled, but where the seemingly intangible often produces the most lasting results, defeat had by no means been complete. Thousands of lives had been profoundly shaped. Through institutions founded and techniques introduced, Americans had left an impress in family and personal ideals, religion, education, medicine, nursing, the natural sciences, engineering, forestry, and agriculture. Communism was by no means the final stage in China's revolution. There would be others, although no one could know what these would be. It was certain that, when China moved into them, that for which Americans had labored would not be entirely lost, but would persist in one way or another. It would be in altered forms, for it would be assimilated into a living, growing China. But it would be there.

Selected Bibliography

The Annals of the American Academy of Political and Social Science, Vol. 277 (Sept., 1951), "Report on China," contains a series of informative articles.

The American Record in the Far East, 1945–1951

A. D. Barnett, "Profile of Red China," *Foreign Policy Reports*, Vol. XXV, No. 19 (Feb. 15, 1950).

J. Belden, *China Shakes the World* (New York: Harper & Brothers, 1949). Strongly critical of the Nationalist regime.

Economic Aid to China Under the China Aid Act of 1948 (Washington: Economic Cooperation Administration, 1949).

J. K. Fairbank, *The United States and China* (Cambridge: Harvard University Press, 1948). An admirable survey.

The Program of the Joint Commission on Rural Reconstruction in China (Washington: Economic Cooperation Administration, 1951).

F. C. Jones, *Manchuria Since 1931* (London: Royal Institute of International Affairs, 1949).

J. F. Ray, *UNRRA in China* (mimeographed—New York: International Secretariat, Institute of Pacific Relations, 1947).

F. W. Riggs, "Chinese Administration in Formosa," *Far Eastern Survey*, Vol. XX, No. 21 (Dec. 12, 1951).

F. W. Riggs, "The Economics of Red China," *Foreign Policy Reports*, Vol. XXVII, No. 6 (June 1, 1951).

L. K. Rosinger and associates, *The State of Asia: A Contemporary Survey* (New York: Alfred A. Knopf, 1951).

United States Relations with China with Special Reference to the Period 1944-1949 (Department of State Publication 3573, Far Eastern Series 30, Aug. 1949). Based on the files of the Department of State.

F. Utley, *The China Story* (Chicago: Henry Regnery Co., 1951). Highly denunciatory of the policy of the Truman Administration.

G. F. Winfield, *China: The Land and the People* (New York: William Sloane Associates, 1948).

Military Situation in the Far East: Hearings Before the Committee on Armed Services and the Committee on Foreign Relations, United States Senate, Eighty-second Congress, First Session, to Conduct an Inquiry into the Military Situation in the Far East and the Facts Surrounding the Relief of General of the Army Douglas MacArthur from His Assignments in That Area (Washington, 5 parts, 1951).

IX. THE RECORD IN JAPAN

IN THE OCCUPATION OF JAPAN THE UNITED STATES
had one of the greatest tests in its history. Here was an episode
which could not have been anticipated at the turn of the century,
and which as late as 1940 would have seemed unthinkable to most
Americans. In 1951 it was too soon to know the outcome. The
record to date could be summarized and appraised; but whether
the final verdict would be success or failure, no one could know
for many years. Yet it was clear that some lasting results would
follow. In the years after V-J Day, Japan entered into one of
the major transitional periods of her long history, comparable
with that which followed the introduction of Buddhism and
Chinese culture fourteen hundred years ago, or to that which was
inaugurated by the coming of Perry in 1853. When these great
movements began no one could have given a precise picture of
the Japan which would emerge from them. Similarly in 1951,
when the transition was in its early stages, no one could foresee
what Japan would be like fifty or a hundred years later. It was
certain, however, that in the occupation of a defeated enemy
country American statesmanship and the American spirit had
undergone a searching examination, and that the outcome would
be momentous for the United States, Japan, the Far East, and
the entire world.

At the outset of our appraisal we can put down a number of
facts as incontestable. We know that the experience had been
unprecedented for both Japan and the United States, that it was
entered upon by the highest American officials with the desire
to serve the people of Japan and the Far East, that it was accepted
and even welcomed by the majority of the Japanese, and that it

was confronted by problems which by their very nature could not be quickly or completely solved.

Never since the dawn of recorded history had Japan been successfully invaded. The original inhabitants must have come from across the sea; but precisely when and how they arrived is in debate. Never since the Japanese had become a self-conscious, civilized people had they been conquered and their land occupied by the victors. They had been taught to believe that theirs was the land of the gods, and that it was inviolable. The shock of disillusion and the mental and moral confusion were great and would have been still greater had it not been for the physical and nervous exhaustion which for many partially numbed sensibilities and induced an approach to apathy.

For the United States the task was also without precedent. In the Philippines and Puerto Rico Americans had attempted to prepare the peoples for democracy; but the populations were much smaller, and neither had a long tradition of independence and nationalism; and, except in the Philippines after World War II, the United States was not confronted with disorganization and exhaustion from a long and destructive war.

The Americans in charge of the occupation came without vindictiveness and with an honest desire to rehabilitate Japan in such a way that it would not again be a menace to the United States or its other neighbors. They wished the Japanese people, freed from the incubus of the militarists who had led them into their mad venture for empire, to have the opportunity to achieve a fair livelihood and develop institutions which would be democratic as Americans defined that word. On the occasion of the formal surrender of Japan on September 2, 1945, General Douglas MacArthur, as Supreme Commander for the Allied Powers, declared:

A new era is upon us. . . . Men since the beginning of time have sought peace. Various methods through the ages have attempted to devise an international process to prevent or settle disputes between nations. . . . We now have our last chance. . . . The problem basically is theological and involves a spiritual recrudescence and improvement of human character that will synchronize with our almost matchless advances in science, art, literature, and all material and cultural developments of the past two thousand years. It must be of the spirit if we are to save the flesh.

We stand in Tokyo today reminiscent of our countryman, Commodore Perry, ninety-two years ago. His purpose was to bring to Japan an era of enlightenment and progress by lifting the veil of isolation to the friendship, trade, and commerce of the world. But alas the knowledge thereby gained of Western science was forged into an instrument of oppression and human enslavement. Freedom of expression, freedom of action, even freedom of thought were denied through suppression of liberal education, through appeal to superstition and through the application of force.

We are committed by the Potsdam Declaration of principles to see that the Japanese people are liberated from this condition of slavery. It is my purpose to implement this commitment just as rapidly as the armed forces are demobilized and the other essential steps taken to neutralize the war potential.

The words were noble. Could they be translated into reality? Traditionally, even at best, occupations have been of mixed value to both the occupied and the occupiers. Would this prove an exception?

As we have suggested, the problems which confronted the occupation were numerous. For most of them no early or easy solution was possible. Some of them were all but insoluble.

There was the ever present pressure of population. It had been one of the causes which had set Japan's feet in the way toward war, and it was aggravated by the outcome of the war. With an area only about the size of the state of California, Japan had to support a population more than half as large as that of the entire United States. Of that area only about a fifth at most could be brought under cultivation. Much of the remainder was forested, and the forest products were important. The waters surrounding the islands teemed with fish; and underneath the soil were some useful minerals, especially coal. Yet in most minerals essential to an industrial civilization Japan was notoriously lacking, especially iron and petroleum. Before the war the Japanese were seeking to meet the situation by becoming a manufacturing and commercial nation. They had acquired much technical skill for modern industries and had used the abundance of cheap labor made available by the surplus of man power. They had developed a merchant marine. Through commerce they had exchanged the products of their factories for food and raw materials. Until their military adventures in China in the 1930's, the average standard of living, while low, was rising, in spite of the burden of a major army and a major navy.

The war and its outcome greatly intensified the country's basic economic problems. The population continued to mount by the excess of births over deaths; indeed, the health measures taken by the occupation widened the margin by lowering the death rate. Population was increasing by something like a million a year, and in 1951 amounted to approximately eighty-four and a half million. Added to the natural increase were the millions of ex-servicemen from the armed forces and the civilians from the overseas possessions who were repatriated after defeat. Most of the commercial fleet, like the navy, had been sunk by enemy action. Industrial plants had been put under terrific pressure to supply the sinews of war, and a large proportion of them had been destroyed or crippled by American bombing. Railways were in bad condition, their equipment gone or badly worn. The soil had been impoverished by inability to obtain enough commercial fertilizer. Forests had been depleted by heavy cutting. The fisheries had been reduced. The areas to which, before defeat, the Japanese had looked for markets and raw materials were now to a large degree cut off.

Manchuria, Korea, and Formosa, which had been geared into Japan's economic structure, were severed from it. China, on whose market and raw materials the Japanese had built large hopes, offered little immediate relief, at first because of the exhaustion and disorder in that land and then because of the Communist triumph and the orientation toward Russia. Throughout the Far East the war had left a heritage of dislike and fear of the Japanese which hampered a resumption of trade. Japan's economic position, grave before the war, had become much more serious at its close.

The Japanese were in poor condition physically and psychologically to cope with the problem. They were undernourished, poorly clad; and a large proportion of the city dwellers had lost their homes through bombing by American planes. They were suffering from the prolonged strain of the war, for the struggle had really begun in September, 1931, and its tempo had mounted as the years wore on. Now they were disillusioned and discouraged. The propaganda on which they had been fed had brought them disaster. They tended to jeer at the returning soldiers rather than to greet them as heroes.

Continued hardship would prepare fertile soil for Communism, which in postwar Japan appealed to many of the students and intelligentsia. Moreover, with so much of the neighboring mainland dominated by Communists, Japan might seek to make some kind of accommodation with them, if only in the interest of trade. Eventually, especially if hardships persisted and the government proved inefficient, Communism might take power.

Still more basic problems confronted the occupation. By tradition going back to their earliest history the Japanese had been a military people. That tradition had been strengthened under the centuries of feudalism and of rule by the Shoguns, whose title signified commander of the military forces. After the end of the shogunate, in 1867, the tradition had been reinforced; and in recent years the fighting services had largely dominated the government. Japan could be disarmed, and for the moment the military were discredited. Would that be permanent? In a world which was armed to the teeth, and in which the armament race was intensified by the tension between the giants, would a people as numerous as the Japanese and with its military history remain unarmed? The answer was almost certainly No.

Could the Japanese really become democratic as Americans understood that word? Again history was adverse. Japanese society was hierarchical. While from time to time explosions had occurred which threatened chaos, such as the assassinations in the 1930's by the younger officers and the attempt, fortunately foiled, to prevent the surrender in 1945 even after it had been decided by the highest authorities, in general the Japanese were a disciplined people, submissive to those in power. They were not accustomed to freedom of speech and assembly and lacked the sense of civic responsibility which is usually developed where these have long been habits. In spite of superficial changes in the last century which seemed revolutionary, certain fundamental institutions or habits of mind persisted and in some cases were even strengthened. One of these was the Emperor and reverence for the throne. Another was the military tradition. Another was the habit of obedience to authority. Even though Americans did not attempt to force on Japan the machinery of democracy to which they were accustomed, could they succeed in transmitting the democratic spirit and habit of mind?

In meeting the problems which stood in the way of its announced purposes, the occupation could count on certain favorable factors. The Japanese had a tradition of willingness and even eagerness to learn from foreigners. Through the centuries they had adopted and adapted much from China. After the coming of Perry they had gone to school to the Occident. They were predisposed to learn from the United States. They had been clearly defeated, for the most part frankly accepted that fact, and sought to learn the secret of the victors' success. Their tradition of submitting to authority favored their acquiescence in what the occupation might command or seek to persuade them to do. The military had been thoroughly discredited, and a large proportion, perhaps the majority, of the Japanese would welcome disarmament and oppose projects for rearming. The Emperor and the imperial family were cooperative and were eager to adapt themselves to the new day in such fashion as would best serve the interests of the Japanese nation. Moreover, the Japanese possessed more industrial know-how than any other people in the Far East. They were a natural center for the industrialization which that area very much needed. They had been relieved of the incubus of the economically unprofitable army and navy.

In general, the initial behavior of the occupying forces was an asset. To the intense surprise of the Japanese, the Americans were not vindictive. There were some unhappy incidents, but in the main the American soldiers were friendly, even kindly. Most of the members of the occupation staff worked hard at their task of remaking Japan. In General MacArthur the occupation had a director who in a remarkable way met the need of the Japanese at that particular time. He had dignity, initiative, a commanding presence, and self-confidence, would not brook insubordination or disloyalty, was hopeful and inspired hope in a dispirited, bewildered people, was hard-working, and gave the Japanese the kind of leadership which they wanted and understood. MacArthur and his subordinates realized, at least in principle, that the Japanese must work out their own salvation, that they must develop their own institutions, and that all that the occupation could do was to clear away some of the obstacles, help in relief and rehabilitation, and give temporary direction toward the attainment of the desired goals. While some important features of the old order were swept aside, the main structure of the accustomed government was preserved. That was notably true of the imperial institution, long the center of stability.

There were in Japan fairly numerous and influential elements who, having studied democratic institutions in the Occident, understood and worked for the adoption and adaptation of democracy. Indeed, in the 1920's, after World War I, when the tide was setting toward democracy in much of the world, Japan had made notable progress in that direction. Some of those who had led in that movement were still living.

As the time passed, conditions in the occupation itself ceased to favor its success. The youthful Americans who were sent to replace the veteran troops sometimes made spectacles of themselves. Arrogance and discourtesy increased, and there were incidents of outright rowdyism. Americans in the occupation, both civilian and military, enjoyed special privileges. Compared with the Japanese, they lived in luxury. While food and some other suppplies were brought in from the United States, local expenses for housing, etc., were charged to the Japanese government, and took from a fifth to a fourth of the national budget. Even before his recall, MacArthur's glamour was waning. By 1951 the occupation was beginning to outlive its usefulness, and resentment against it was rising.

The chief outlines of the machinery through which the occupation operated can be quickly described. The occupation was predominantly American. Some other powers which had shared in inflicting the defeat sent small contingents of troops and a few administrators and technicians; but the overwhelming majority of the personnel came from the United States, and actually, although not in theory, the direction was American. MacArthur, an American, was Supreme Commander for the Allied Powers, and the structure of which he was the head was, accordingly, known as SCAP.

In principle MacArthur was to act under the direction of the

Far Eastern Commission. This body, set up on the basis of an agreement reached at Moscow in December, 1945, by the United States, the U.S.S.R., and Great Britain (China concurring), was composed of representatives of eleven countries which had joined in defeating Japan—the U.S.S.R., Great Britain, the United States, China, France, the Netherlands, Canada, Australia, New Zealand, India, and the Philippines. To them were added in November, 1947, Burma and Pakistan. Yet its headquarters were at Washington, and in general its decisions did little more than confirm policies already adopted and put into practice by the United States. On June 19, 1947, it adopted a basic policy statement differing only in detail from the initial post-surrender policy toward Japan which had been framed by the State, War, and Navy departments and approved by President Truman on September 6, 1945.

The Moscow conference also set up the Allied Council in Tokyo. On it were representatives of the U.S.S.R., China, the British Commonwealth of Nations, and the United States. General MacArthur was its chairman; but he attended only its first session, being represented at others by a deputy. The Allied Council had only advisory powers. Although its sessions were sometimes stormy, General MacArthur's will always prevailed, and in the end it became largely inactive.

Under the policy decision adopted by the Far Eastern Commission in June, 1947, the basic object of SCAP was to ensure that Japan would "not again become a menace to the peace and security of the world," and "to bring about the earliest possible establishment of a democratic and peaceful government which will carry out its international responsibilities, respect the rights of other states, and support the objectives of the United Nations. Such government in Japan should be established in accordance with the freely expressed will of the Japanese people."

147

These objectives [the directive went on to say] will be achieved by the following principal means:

Japan's sovereignty will be limited to the islands of Honshu, Hokkaido, Kyushu, Shikoku, and such minor islands as may be determined.

Japan will be completely disarmed and demilitarized. The authority of the militarists and the influence of militarism will be totally eliminated. All institutions expressive of the spirit of militarism and aggression will be vigorously suppressed.

The Japanese people shall be encouraged to develop a desire for individual liberties and respect for fundamental human rights, particularly the freedoms of religion, assembly and association, speech and the press. They shall be encouraged to form democratic and representative organizations.

Japan shall be permitted to maintain such industries as will sustain her economy and permit the exaction of just reparations in kind, but not those which would enable her to rearm for war. To this end access to, as distinguished from control of, raw materials should be permitted. Eventual Japanese participation in world trade relations will be permitted.

The authority of the Emperor and the Japanese government was to be subject to the Supreme Commander. He was to exercise his authority through Japanese governmental machinery and agencies, including the Emperor, but only to the extent which would further the objectives of the directive.

We can give here only the briefest summary of what was accomplished under SCAP in the six years between the dramatic scene on the *Missouri* on September 2, 1945, when the formal surrender of Japan was signed, and the equally impressive signing of the peace treaty in San Francisco on September 8, 1951. A vast literature has already appeared of official reports and comprehensive surveys. More will be coming in the years ahead. However, our appraisal of the American record in the Far East, cursory though it is, must attempt to list the main acts of the occupation and to estimate their effectiveness.

Sweeping measures were adopted to demilitarize Japan and to

eliminate the influence of militarism and supernationalism. The imperial army and navy were disbanded, and steps were taken to purge from public life all persons who had advocated doctrines of militarism and imperialism. State Shinto was abolished, thus striking at the religious roots of aggressive nationalism. On January 1, 1946, the Emperor issued a rescript in which he declared that the long cherished conception of his divinity which had been inculcated through many channels was false, and branded as untrue the associated teaching that the Japanese were superior to other peoples and were destined to rule mankind. That same month MacArthur commanded the Japanese government to dissolve the various military and patriotic organizations, such as the Black Dragon Society, which had been advocates and bulwarks of militarism and imperialism. A few days earlier the teaching of history, geography, and morals in the schools was suspended, for here had been one of the chief means by which youth had been indoctrinated with chauvinism. The teaching staffs of the nation were screened, and thousands were eliminated as tainted with militaristic sentiments. New textbooks were produced, and before the end of 1946 the teaching of geography and history was resumed.

Looking in the same direction was the trial of former Japanese officials who were accused of leading the nation into war and of crimes against humanity in the conduct of the war. An international tribunal was set up to try the major "war criminals," including former Prime Minister Tojo. A prolonged trial was conducted amid great publicity, and in November, 1948, a verdict of guilty was handed down for twenty-five, seven of whom were condemned to death. Within a few weeks several had been executed, an appeal to the Supreme Court of the United States having proved unsuccessful. By the end of 1951 a number of those imprisoned as war criminals had been released.

Steps were taken to dissolve the *zaibatsu*, the huge family combinations of capital through which much of the industry, banking, commerce, and shipping had been conducted. They had been closely associated with Japan's imperialistic ventures and, during the war, had been emphatically denounced by many Americans as part of the system which produced aggression. The five largest of the *zaibatsu* were forced to turn over to a Holding Company Liquidation Commission their shares in the corporations which they controlled and to accept in exchange government bonds which were not to be sold for ten years.

The attempt was made further to give permanence to the demilitarization of Japan in the new constitution, produced under somewhat insistent proddings from SCAP. Outwardly the procedures were those prescribed in the old constitution of 1889, which provided that changes were to be initiated at the command of the Emperor and must be submitted to the Diet. In the autumn of 1945 the Japanese addressed themselves to the problem, but the initial results were not satisfactory to SCAP. The new constitution was based on a draft prepared in General MacArthur's headquarters, and strong pressure was brought to bear on the Japanese to induce them to accept SCAP's ideas. It was promulgated by the Emperor over the radio on November 3, 1946, and went into effect in May, 1947. Its ninth article declared that "the Japanese people renounce war as a sovereign right of the nation and the threat or use of force as means of settling international disputes. . . . Land, sea, and air forces, as well as other war potential, will never be maintained. The right of belligerency of the state will not be recognized."

The provisions of the new constitution were emphatically democratic. The preamble began: "We, the Japanese people . . . proclaim that sovereign power resides with the people. . . . Government is a sacred trust of the people, the authority for which is derived from the people, the powers of which are exercised by the representatives of the people, and the benefits of which are enjoyed by the people." The emperor was to be the symbol of the state, "deriving his position from the will of the people."

The people were not to be prevented from enjoying "any of the fundamental human rights." There was to be "no discrimination in political, economic, or social relations, because of race, creed, sex, social status or family origin." "Universal adult suffrage" was guaranteed. The state was to "refrain from religious education or any other religious activity," thus making unconstitutional a revival of State Shinto. Freedom of thought, conscience, religion, assembly and association, speech, press and all other forms of expression, of the choice and change of residence, and of choice of occupation were guaranteed. No censorship was to be maintained, nor was the secrecy of any means of communication to be violated. There was to be no involuntary servitude except as punishment for crime. All were to have "the right to maintain the minimum standards of wholesome and cultured living . . . to receive an equal education correspondent to their ability . . . the right and the obligation to work." "The right of workers to organize and bargain and act collectively" was guaranteed. The right to own and hold property was declared inviolate. All were to have access to the courts. No one was to "be arrested or detained without being at once informed of the charges against him or without the immediate privilege of counsel; nor shall he be detained without adequate cause." "The infliction of torture by any public officer and cruel punishments" were forbidden. No one was to be compelled to testify against himself. The highest organ of state power was declared to be the Diet, and both houses were to "consist of elected members, representative of all the people."

Legislation subsequent to the promulgation of the constitution made members of the imperial family subject to the laws of Japan in their status as private citizens. Legislation also effected a considerable degree of decentralization of political authority, giving more power to local units, providing for the election of local assemblymen and heads of prefectures, cities, towns, and villages. The Police Reorganization Law of December, 1947, decentralized the police system and thus deprived the Tokyo government of one of the means which the military had used to enforce conformity with their wishes. Police were trained in democratic methods.

A sweeping agrarian reorganization was carried through as the result of pressure from SCAP. About half the population lived on farms, and about 75 per cent of the farm population were tenants. For many years the status of the tenants had been highly unsatisfactory, and the occupation authorities acted to improve their lot. In 1946 legislation was passed which provided that the government should buy the holdings of the landlords, which should then be sold to tenants on terms which the latter could afford, and which would enable them to keep their land in times of agricultural depression. Somewhat similarly, in December, 1949, the Diet enacted a measure which ended the fishing rights of absentee owners and made free the grounds for about a million fishermen. This was of major importance, for fish is a major item in the Japanese menu.

The occupation gave attention not only to the farmers and fishermen, but also to the urban workers. The constitution guaranteed the right of laborers to organize, and encouragement was given to the formation of labor unions. As a result unions mushroomed and there was an epidemic of strikes, some of them fomented by Communists. Machinery for conciliation, mediation, and arbitration was set up to promote peaceful adjustment of labor disputes, and government employees were forbidden by law to strike. New laws were passed to assure higher standards of wages and working conditions, and a Labor Ministry was established for the first time.

SCAP and the United States wrestled with the economic problems of Japan. In 1947 industrial production was less than half of that in the first half of the 1930's. Measured by Asian standards, though not by those of the West, taxes were high, as they had been by tradition; but also they were widely evaded. As was to be expected, inflation was mounting, for the government was using the printing press to meet the wide margin between income and expenditure. To aid the situation the United States took money of its own taxpayers and came to the rescue of its late enemies. Between the surrender of Japan and the signing of the peace treaty the United States government spent about $1,800,-000,000 to provide Japan with food and other essential materials.

Obviously Americans would not continue these subsidies indefinitely. In spite of warnings from the United States, the Japanese government, finding reliance on the American treasury easy, did little to put its economic house in order. In May, 1948, the United States sent out a commission headed by Ralph A. Young of the Federal Reserve Board. It recommended a strict economic stabilization program, with wage, price, and credit controls, increased tax collections, and the reduction of government deficit spending. Some slight progress was made, but the Japanese government did not take the drastic measures urged by SCAP. In December, 1948, the United States issued a directive to SCAP instructing it to employ stronger methods. The Japanese government then fell into line, and was aided by the firm and wise counsel of Joseph M. Dodge, a Detroit banker appointed by President Truman as financial adviser to General MacArthur.

For the year 1949–1950 the Japanese national budget was brought into balance for the first time in eighteen years, and a single general rate of exchange was established which put pressure on manufacturers to bring their costs into line with world costs and prices.

In June, 1949, an American tax commission headed by Carl S. Shoup outlined measures for improving the tax structure which were to a large extent adopted by SCAP and the Japanese government. By 1951 economic recovery had progressed so far that the United States discontinued its subsidies to Japan although at the same time, in order to cushion the blow, it assumed some of the occupation costs formerly borne by the Japanese government. The Japanese hoped to attract American capital to help rebuild their industries, but because of the hazards and difficulties involved, and the more attractive opportunities at home, very few American funds had been invested in Japan at the time the peace treaty was signed.

In 1949 the United States terminated the payment of reparations by Japan on the ground that they obstructed the stabilization of the Japanese economy. Machinery valued at about $35,-000,000 had been shipped on reparations account to China, the Philippines, the Netherlands, and Great Britain. In addition, Japan's overseas assets, valued at about $3,000,000,000 (of which two-thirds was in China) had been confiscated as reparations.

The educational system of Japan was thoroughly reorganized. Not only were elements eliminated which had contributed to militarization and imperialism, but more sweeping changes were made. These came as the result of the findings of the United States Education Mission in March, 1946, embodied a year later in a comprehensive educational program of the Far Eastern Commission. Education, the Far Eastern Commission directed, was "to be looked upon as the pursuit of truth and as preparation for life in a democratic nation." Educational opportunities were to be broadened, uniform minimum standards of excellence were to be set up, and control was to be decentralized. Compulsory, tuition-free primary education was to be increased from the existing six years to nine years, the number and capacity of colleges and universities were to be augmented, with equal opportunity for all, regardless of sex or social position, and curriculums were to be expanded and liberalized. These changes were embodied in the Education Standards Law of March, 1947, the Education Committee Law of July, 1948, and the Education Ministry Establishment Law of 1949. Partly on the American pattern, parent-teacher associations were organized in many parts of the country. In addition, at American expense, scores of Japanese scholars and educators were sent to the United States to observe methods and to study in the fields of their specialization.

Nongovernmental American agencies also assisted in the postwar rehabilitation of Japan. The Christians of the United States, both Protestant and Roman Catholic, contributed extensively to the physical relief of individuals and groups. They also perceived in the groping of Japanese for inner security after their disillusionment with nationalistic propaganda an unsurpassed open-mindedness to the Christian message. As a result, numbers of missionaries returned, and hundreds of new ones were sent out.

As the years passed, the problem of a peace treaty with Japan became more and more urgent. It was clear from the beginning that the occupation must be temporary. To prolong it would be bad for both Japanese and Americans, because it would lead to continued dependence, irritation, and a sense of outraged futility among the former and would make for moral deterioration among the latter. But the occupation could not well be terminated before relations between Japan and the United States had once more been placed on a treaty basis.

A single treaty between Japan and all her former enemies would have been desirable. Yet it proved impracticable, for the growing rift between Russia and the United States made agreement between these two powers all but impossible. For instance, in 1947, the United States attempted to assemble a conference in which the eleven states which were members of the Far Eastern Commission would be represented; but the U.S.S.R. insisted that the peace treaty with Japan be considered first by the Council of Foreign Ministers, and to this Washington could not agree. After the Communists gained control of China, and especially after they intervened in the Korean War, Chinese participation in drafting a treaty for Japan was complicated by the existence of two rival Chinese governments, one backed by Russia and the other by the United States.

Obviously the United States was under the necessity of giving some kind of leadership. In May, 1950, the Department of State announced that John Foster Dulles had been asked to give special attention to "problems concerning a Japanese peace settlement," and President Truman said that he hoped that a treaty was not too far distant. In September, 1950, President Truman reported that discussions would be undertaken with the other governments represented on the Far Eastern Commission. Dulles soon began a round of conversations with representatives of these governments in New York and Washington and also with representatives of Ceylon and Indonesia. The conversations included the Russians, and for a time it seemed that the U.S.S.R. might be conciliatory.

However, it soon became apparent that accord between Russia and the United States was not to be reached. In the fall of 1950, Dulles submitted a memorandum as a basis for discussion with representatives of the other governments on the Far Eastern Commission. In November, Moscow raised a number of objections. Chou En-lai, speaking for the People's Republic of China, demanded that his government be permitted to share in the negotiations and condemned the American proposals. On May 7, 1951, Moscow renewed its earlier insistence that the treaty with Japan be drawn up by the Council of Foreign Ministers of the Big Four—Great Britain, the United States, the U.S.S.R., and China (i.e. the People's Republic). The note also sharply attacked the American approach as designed to impose the will of the United States on Japan and as excluding the Soviet Union, China, and other countries from full participation. On May 20, 1951, this procedure was formally rejected by the United States. In view of the fact that, largely on the initiative of the United States, the People's Republic had been declared an aggressor in Korea, that the United States had never recognized it as the government of China, and that discussions with Russia over peace treaties in Europe, notably Austria and Germany, had failed of agreement, this decision was to be expected.

Early in 1951 Dulles went to Japan and had conversations with the leaders of the government as well as representatives of political parties, business, labor, and other important groups. In an address on February 2, he said that the United States would be willing to keep forces in or near Japan but only if the Japanese wished them. Polls showed that the large majority of the Japanese desired them, and that only about a sixth were opposed. He went on to the Philippines, Australia, and New Zealand to discuss the treaty. His purpose in these other countries was to allay misunderstandings and fears, especially of Japan, to win their accord, and to arrive at agreements for common defense in the Pacific.

The removal by President Truman of General MacArthur as Supreme Commander for the Allied Powers on April 11, 1951, of which we shall have more to say in the next chapter, and the appointment of General Matthew B. Ridgway, did not seriously affect either the occupation of Japan or the negotiations for the treaty of peace. At the moment, the suddenness of the step produced something akin to consternation in Japan, because to the Japanese people MacArthur had symbolized the occupation and had given a sense of stability and security in what at the outset threatened chaos. However, the progress of recovery in Japan had rendered him less essential, and interest in him had been declining. Indeed, the recall of MacArthur was salutary for Japan, as a demonstration that in American democracy the civilian authorities were in control and could not be browbeaten or overridden by the military. The opposite of this had been the undoing of Japan. Moreover, the United States government made it clear that the step did not indicate any change in its policy toward Japan.

Partly to reassure the Japanese, Dulles was immediately asked to go to Japan to continue the negotiations about the treaty on the basis of the earlier conversations. He complied, and then, after a few weeks in the United States, he went to England and France to win their accord.

In drafting the treaty care was taken not to provoke unnecessary resentment among the Japanese. Japan was to be restored as a sovereign state, equal with other sovereign states and not under permanent restrictions or disabilities which would make her different from any other free nation. It was meant to effect reconciliation and to carry out the generous purposes of the occupation. To do otherwise would have created bitterness which, like the punitive features of the Treaty of Versailles in the case of Germany after World War I, could become a grievance exploited by agitators to the detriment of the peace.

To be sure, the terms of the Potsdam Proclamation of July, 1945, under which Japan had surrendered, called for limitation of the territory of the empire to the islands of Honshu, Hokkaido, Kyushu, and Shikoku, and "such minor islands" as the Allies might determine. Accordingly the treaty mainly confined Japan to these four islands. In pursuance of the Yalta decisions of February, 1945, Russia was already in possession of the southern half of Sakhalin, the Kuriles, and some of the Japanese holdings in Manchuria. Under the treaty, Japan renounced her rights in Sakhalin and the Kuriles; but these were not explicitly given to Russia. Similarly she divested herself of all her "right, title and claim to Formosa and the Pescadores," but with no statement as to their future ownership. The Cairo Declaration, it will be recalled, had promised them to "the Republic of China."

Japan also surrendered her claims to the islands in the Pacific which she held under mandate from the League of Nations and agreed to the action of the United Nations Security Council of April 2, 1947, which placed them under United States trusteeship. Japan renounced all claims in the Antarctic region and to the Paracel and Spratly islands. She agreed to "concur in any proposal of the United States to the United Nations to place under its trusteeship system, with the United States as the sole administering authority, the Nansei Shoto south of 29° north latitude, (including the Ryukyu Islands and the Daito Islands), Nanpo Shoto south of Sofu Gan (including the Bonin Islands, Rosario Island, and the Volcano Islands) and Parece Vela and Marcus Island." Pending the making of such a proposal and affirmative action thereon, the United States was to "have the right to exercise all and any powers of administration, legislation, and jurisdiction over the territory and inhabitants of these islands, including their territorial waters." It may be added that, having taken them during World War II, the United States was already in possession. Okinawa especially had been fortified. However, in contrast with what had formerly been customary for victors in a war and in accordance with its commitment to the United Nations, instead of annexing them outright, the United States was prepared to hold the islands as trustee for the United Nations and under such terms as should be approved by that body.

Unique provisions were included both to prevent a freed Japan from waging a war of revenge or renewing her aggression and to protect her against possibly aggressive neighbors. Although the treaty could not make Japan a member of the United Nations (a step which Russia would probably veto), yet Japan accepted the obligations set forth in Article 2 of the Charter of the United Nations and in particular the obligations

i. to settle its international disputes by peaceful means in such a manner that international peace and security, and justice, are not endangered;

ii. to refrain in its international relations from the threat or use of force against the territorial integrity or political independence of any State or in any other manner inconsistent with the purposes of the United Nations;

iii. to give the United Nations every assistance in any action it takes in accordance with the Charter and to refrain from giving assistance to any State against which the United Nations may take preventive or enforcement action.

In return, the other signatories to the treaty declared that they would be guided by the principles of Article 2 of the Charter in their relations with Japan, that they recognized "that Japan as a sovereign nation possesses the inherent right of individual or collective self-defense referred to in Article 51 of the Charter of the United Nations and that Japan may voluntarily enter into collective security arrangements."

All occupation forces were to be withdrawn from Japan at least ninety days after the coming into force of the treaty; but the treaty was not to "prevent the stationing or retention of foreign armed forces in Japanese territory under or in consequence of any bilateral or multilateral agreements which have been or may be made between one or more of the Allied Powers, on the one hand, and Japan on the other."

Thus the defense of Japan, the possibility of her rearming, and safeguards against a renewal of aggression by her were assured, so far as that could be done by treaty. Spokesmen for the People's Republic of China and the U.S.S.R. were loud in their denunciations of what they asserted was the rearming of Japan by the United States. Some other Pacific countries were apprehensive, though lesss vocally. Yet to withdraw all armed forces from Japan and to deny her the privilege of rearming would expose her to almost certain occupation by Russia or Communist China, although probably under the guise of a government set up by Japanese Communists. To leave Japan completely free might permit a renewal of aggression on her part. She was, then, drawn within the structure of the obligations of the Charter of the United Nations.

In the treaty Japan declared her willingness to enter into negotiations with each of the Allied Powers for commercial treaties, and pending conclusion of such treaties to accord to each of the Allied Powers and their citizens most-favored-nation treatment, but only in case she was assured similar treatment. In other words, the principle of equality was adopted.

The thorny problem of reparations was handled by recognizing that, although in principle Japan should pay them, she lacked the capacity to do so in full, to meet her other obligations, and to maintain a viable economy. It was provided that Japan would enter promptly into negotiations with such of the Allied Powers as desired it "with a view to assisting to compensate those countries for the cost of repairing the damage done, by making available the services of the Japanese people in production, salvaging, and other work for the Allied Powers in question"; but such arrangements were to "avoid the imposition of additional liabilities on other Allied Powers," thus safeguarding against indirect payment by the United States, nor were they to throw any additional exchange burden on Japan.

There were also provisions for the meeting by Japan of her prewar obligations abroad, for restoration or compensation for property taken from citizens of states while at war, and for the legalization of the seizure, retention, or liquidation of Japanese property in former enemy countries with certain important and specifically named exceptions.

The United States did not quickly or easily win all other governments to its views. As we have seen, Russia, although approached, proposed another procedure to which the United States would not assent. Great Britain wished a more severe treaty, largely because she feared Japanese competition in the markets of the world, notably in cotton textiles and shipping. Some others had fears of renewed aggression if Japan were permitted to recover and especially if she were allowed to rearm. Some were unhappy over the failure to exact reparations more nearly commensurate with the damage they had suffered from Japan. Yet the United States succeeded in persuading nearly all the non-Communist countries to accept substantially its point of view, and except for some details the treaty followed the outline originally suggested by the American government. The final drafts of the treaty were made after consultation with Great Britain and were sponsored jointly by that country and the United States. Care was taken to confer with other Asiatic states, especially India, Pakistan, and Indonesia, to take account of their peculiar interest in Far Eastern affairs.

From the invitations sent out to fifty-four countries to join in San Francisco on September 4, 1951, in the signing of the treaty, both the regimes claiming to speak for China—namely, that of the Communists and that of the Nationalists—were conspicuous by their omission. In August, India recommended certain modifications in the treaty. She thought that the document should specify the return of Formosa to China, that Japan should be allowed to keep the Ryukyu and Bonin islands, and that any arrangements for stationing American troops in Japan should be made after Japan had regained full sovereignty. India, together with Burma, declined to attend the San Francisco conference. Yet on September 8, 1951, the treaty was signed by the representatives of Japan and forty-eight other nations. It was a notable occasion for Japan and a signal victory for the diplomacy of the United States.

Care had been taken to consult both Democrats and Republicans in the Congress, and especially in the Senate. It was to the Senate that the treaty would come for ratification, and failure there would set back formal peace with Japan an indefinite period.

The treaty of peace with Japan was supplemented by defense agreements with the Philippines, Australia, and New Zealand, which went far to relieve the apprehension felt in these countries over possible future aggression by Japan. On August 30, 1951, the United States and the Philippines signed a new mutual security pact, and on September 1, 1951, a similar treaty was concluded by the United States with Australia and New Zealand. On September 8, 1951, representatives of the United States and Japan affixed their signatures to a treaty which gave the United States the right to maintain its forces in and near Japan for an indefinite period. The document said that Japan would "increasingly assume responsibility for its own defense," but would avoid weapons "which could be an offensive threat." The treaty imposed no commitments on the United States to defend Japan. All these treaties, especially that with Japan, were thought of as preliminary steps toward a broader Pacific security agreement which might be negotiated in the future. On February 28, 1952, an administrative agreement was signed at Tokyo by the United States and Japan to implement the security treaty between the two countries. It specified in detail the relations of the two governments and the status of the armed forces and the associated civilians who were to be placed in Japan in pursuance of the treaty.

On April 28, 1952, the peace treaty, having been ratified by eleven countries, including Japan and the United States, was formally proclaimed by President Truman. The Japanese-American security treaty went into effect at the same time.

Striking as was the diplomatic achievement of the United States, it was not an unqualified victory. Russia refused to sign the treaty. The People's Republic of China was not represented, but Japan would have to reckon with that country as a near and powerful neighbor whose trade she badly needed. India and Burma declined to send representatives to San Francisco. The treaty was intensely unpopular in the Philippines, partly because it did not grant that country the reparations which its people believed to be their due. Some Filipinos felt that the United States was more generous to Japan, its former enemy, than to the Philippines, its friend. Many were fearful of the rearming of a nation from whose aggression they had recently suffered so severely and, in view of the failure of the United States to save them from invasion by Japan in 1941, were distrustful of the value of the new joint defense pact between the two countries. In Japan itself there was strong sentiment against relinquishing the Ryukyu and Bonin islands.

The conclusion of the treaties with Japan marked the termination of an important stage in the postwar relations of that country with the United States. It was a good time to take stock and to essay a tentative appraisal of the success or failure of the occupation.

Here had been an amazing experiment. In its occupation of Japan the United States, far from being vindictive, had attempted to put its late enemy on its feet, and while preventing it from being a menace to others and to itself, to set it on the road to recovery and to equality among the nations of the world, to enable it to make a livelihood, to remedy some of its basic ills, and to work toward a democratic government and society.

As we have said, the experiment had been undertaken from a mixture of motives. One was self-interest. The United States wanted never again to have to go to war to stop an aggressive Japan. Nor did the United States wish Japan to be so weak that she would fall into the arms of the hereditary enemy of the island empire, Russia. If Russia were to fulfill her ambition and control both Japan and western Europe with their industrial equipment and skills, she would acquire a marked and perhaps an overwhelming advantage in her struggle with the United States. Yet there was much more than self-interest. General MacArthur and the majority of his subordinates, together with the highest authorities in Washington, were genuinely eager to aid the Japanese people to free themselves from the militarists who had brought them to so sad a pass and to help them to build institutions which would ensure a livelihood and freedom. It was with this in mind that they labored. In their efforts there was something of paternalism, the long-standing attitude of the white man toward the colored peoples, a conscious assumption of the "white man's burden." Yet there was good will toward the Japanese and an appreciation of the fact that ultimately the success or failure of the experiment would rest with them.

As to the elimination of the military and militarism the future was by no means clear. The majority of the people were frankly tired of war; and, so far as a constitution could do it, further resort to arms had been ruled out. Yet, living in a world where the two leading powers were arming to the teeth, and where she was on a front line between the two, it was difficult to believe that Japan would remain unarmed. If once she began to rearm, the military might again raise their heads. Japan would long be too weak to be as formidable as she had been in 1941; but her leaders might bargain for concessions from the rivals in return for her support. It may have been ominous that none of those tried and condemned for war guilt seemed to have any sense of moral turpitude, and that the nation at large, while not regarding them as martyred heroes, did not condemn them.

Even more serious was the threat of Communism. The democratic spirit and attitude and democratic institutions as Americans conceive them are things of slow growth. During the 1920's substantial progress had been made. After 1945 thousands were eager to learn what democracy meant, and marked advances were made in setting up the legal framework for it. Yet old traditions died hard. The pre-1941 political parties had been notorious for corruption. That had been one of the reasons urged by the militarists, especially the younger officers, for a political revolution which would eliminate them. In the postsurrender years the prewar parties had disappeared, but the new ones were to a large degree their successors. Many of the prewar politicians were still active. Among them were men of public spirit and integrity; but they were probably in the minority.

In the meantime Communism was present. Communists were only a small proportion of the population, but Communism does not need to have a majority to take over. Where it has come to power it has been by a small, highly disciplined minority who have infiltrated existing organizations or have taken advantage of division and weakness among their opponents and of bad economic and social conditions. In some ways the situation in Japan favored Communism. Communism was skillful in its propaganda. It directed its appeal to students and women, workers and farmers. It brought into being thousands of cells and many Communist front organizations. It was firmly rooted in small and fanatical minorities. If economic conditions deteriorated or did not improve rapidly enough, Communists might achieve the mastery, much as the fanatical militarists had seized the occasion of the world-wide depression of the 1930's to offer their way as the panacea and impose their will on the nation.

Fortunately there were factors which might effectively offset the Communist danger. The Communists were few, were not fully united (some of them held views that were displeasing to Moscow), and they had alienated important elements in Japan. In Japan there was widespread fear of Russia which went back many years; and that distrust had been heightened by the cynical and completely selfish fashion in which the Soviet Union had broken the neutrality pact and had entered the war against Japan when the latter was clearly defeated (although Russia could claim in extenuation that the United States and others had urged this course). Yet with most of the mainland opposite Japan Communist, the pressure on her to conform, for purposes of trade if for no other reason, would be heavy. This was particularly the case because of the importance to Japan of China, both as a market and as a source of raw materials. Trade with China, including Manchuria, seemed to be essential if Japan was to solve her economic problem. Communist China might dictate terms which Japan would feel that she must meet or starve.

Democratic processes in labor had hard sledding, for here the Japanese had had much less experience than in government. SCAP was committed to the organization of labor unions; but they were easy targets of the radicals, and for a time Communist infiltration made headway. SCAP was embarrassed, and curtailed some of the rights of labor to which it was in theory committed, and also curtailed the freedom of the press. This was partly because MacArthur himself was intolerant of criticism, but some such steps would probably have been taken by anyone in charge of the occupation.

A major asset in the struggle against Communism was the imperial institution. To be sure, the Emperor had disavowed his divinity and that of his house. Yet reverence for him was great, partly as an individual but chiefly for his office. The imperial house and the imperial institution were clearly anti-Communist. They might, however, at some future time become a menace to democracy and a support of revived militarism. If the militarists again raised their heads, they would profess to act on behalf of the Emperor. As had been done in Japan for centuries, they would seek to obtain his endorsement, by constraint if necessary, and carry through their program in his name.

On paper the reconstruction of education in Japan was moving forward. However, in the last analysis success or failure depended on the teachers, and the training in democratic ideals of the tens of thousands who would guide youth in their school days could not be quickly accomplished.

In general, the reorganization of Japan's economic structure to rid it of historic inequities was going well. The distribution of land among the actual cultivators had been accomplished. Here and there former landlords managed to retain an undue proportion of their holdings by having members of their families acquire tracts, but in the main the measure was carried through with striking success.

The attempt to dislodge the *zaibatsu* was less effective. The public was slow to buy up the shares offered through the Holding Company Liquidation Commission, and the system of managing the business of the country by huge aggregations of capital closely allied to the state was in danger of reappearing, if not in the pre-surrender pattern, then in other ways. Yet the resumption of the close tie with the state and a resurgent imperialism in which that would play a part was by no means inevitable.

In spite of the work of the Dodge Commission, the financial structure of the government remained insecure. Progress had been made toward a balanced budget, but whether it would continue was not yet certain.

By the close of 1951 distinct advances had been made toward economic recovery. Living standards were below those of the early 1930's, but higher than those of 1945. The domestic production of food was a tenth larger than in 1930–1934. Foreign trade was being revived, although imports still greatly exceeded exports. The war in Korea proved a boon, for many of the needed supplies were produced in Japan and paid for by American money. These shots in the arm were not entirely wholesome, but Japan was also making gains in peacetime exports. She was resuming ship-building and selling the ships, and she was adding to her own merchant marine and therefore to her earning capacity.

Japan's economic future was still precarious. Her population continued to mount, partly because of the success of SCAP through its public health and welfare measures in keeping down the death rate. Former markets and sources of raw materials were cut off by the political situation in China and by the impoverishment which the war, largely of Japan's own doing, had wrought in China and southeast Asia. Before the war Korea had been a source of rice for Japan. Now it was importing rice. In default of other sources, Japan was importing high-priced cereals from the United States.

Yet the outlook was by no means entirely dark. The Japanese were industrious and were beginning to recover their courage and optimism. They had more experience in modern industry than any other people in east or southeast Asia. In spite of the wear and tear of war, destruction by bombing, and obsolescence, Japan possessed more industrial equipment than any other people in east Asia and perhaps all Asia. If China continued to be closed, markets and supplies of raw materials might be found in southeast Asia.

On the whole, judged from the limited perspective of 1951, the achievement of the American occupation in Japan had been remarkable and encouraging. Failures, mistakes, and shortcomings were not lacking, and continued advance in the path in which the United States had tried to set Japan's feet was by no means certain. Yet progress there had been, and enduring and growing success was distinctly possible. Much that Americans had done would pass. The Japanese would discard some, adapt what they retained, and add to it in their own way. But it was distinctly conceivable that the Japanese had permanently joined the ranks of those peoples who were democratic as the United States and the British Commonwealth understood that term.

Selected Bibliography

W. M. Ball, *Japan, Enemy or Ally?* (New York: John Day Co., 1949).

J. W. Ballantine, "Democratic Forces in Prewar Japan," *Far Eastern Survey*, Vol. XX, No. 11 (May 30, 1951).

R. Brines, *MacArthur's Japan* (Philadelphia: J. B. Lippincott Co., 1948).

C. A. Buss, "United States Policy on the Japan Treaty," *Far Eastern Survey,* Vol. XX, No. 12 (June 13, 1951).

M. S. Farley, "Japan and U.S.: Post-Treaty Problems," *Far Eastern Survey,* Vol. XXI, No. 4 (Feb. 27, 1952).

R. A. Fearey, *The Occupation of Japan, Second Phase: 1948–50* (New York: The Macmillan Co., 1950).

M. Gayn, *Japan Diary* (New York: William Sloane Associates, 1948).

E. M. Martin, *The Allied Occupation of Japan* (New York: American Institute of Pacific Relations, 1948).

E. O. Reischauer, *The United States and Japan* (Cambridge: Harvard University Press, 1950).

E. G. Seidensticker, "Japanese Views on Peace," *Far Eastern Survey,* Vol. XX, No. 12 (June 13, 1951).

R. B. Textor, *Failure in Japan, with Keystones for a Positive Policy* (New York: John Day Co., 1951).

Political Reorientation of Japan: September 1945–September 1948 (2 vols., Washington: Government Printing Office, 1950). Report of Government Section, Supreme Commander for the Allied Powers.

x. TRAGEDY IN KOREA, AND

THE GREAT AMERICAN DEBATE

IN KOREA AT THE TIME OF THE SURRENDER OF JAPAN
the United States was faced by an extraordinarily difficult problem to which no easy or early solution was possible, and where
the odds were distinctly against success. In Korea there arose, in
1950, a major crisis which tested both the United States and the
United Nations, and which precipitated in the United States a
major debate over foreign policy.

The difficulties in Korea arose partly from geography and partly
from history. Korea has the misfortune to be a peninsula so
situated between powerful neighbors that it has been a bone of
contention among them. Jutting out from the mainland of Asia,
it commands sea approaches to northern China, Manchuria,
eastern Siberia, and Japan. In the possession of Russia, China, or
Japan, it can be the basis of a threat to the other two. Before the
nineteenth century Chinese influence was dominant, but from
time to time both Japan and China had occupied portions of the
country, China in the north and Japan in the south, and in the
1590's the ambitious Hideyoshi attempted a Japanese invasion
of China by way of Korea. In 1894–1895 Japan and China fought
over Korea. Japan won, but was in turn threatened by Russia.
The Russo-Japanese War of 1904–1905 broke out primarily because of a conflict of interest in Korea. After that war, Japan annexed it and administered it until her defeat in 1945. The Russian,
Chinese, and Japanese empires touched one another on the north-
eastern corner of Korea. In 1938 fighting broke out in that corner,
apparently from an effort by the Japanese to test the Russian de-

fense. The Japanese found it so strong that they did not press the attack.

For several generations the Korean record in self-government had not been good. Earlier Korea had had glorious periods of creative vigor, especially from the eighth to the twelfth century and from the fifteenth to the seventeenth century. From the seventeenth to the nineteenth century the kingdom was independent, except for a vassalage to China which entailed no control over its domestic affairs; but its government was incompetent. Attempts at improvement came to nought. The decrepit regime could not offer effective resistance to the encroachments of its neighbors or to the eventual annexation by Japan. Under the Japanese the Koreans were utilized only in subordinate posts and were not given the increased responsibilities which prepared Indians under British rule for independence.

Nationalism touched the Koreans as it did other peoples of the world. Underground resistance to Japan was effectively curbed in Korea itself, but independence movements were maintained outside the country; there was, however, no unity among them. There was a strong Communist movement, and after 1919 a non-Communist group laboring for independence had maintained itself in China.

Before 1945 American contacts with Korea had been partly through diplomacy but chiefly through missionaries. The United States, as we have seen, had a share in opening Korea to the Western world. Yet President Theodore Roosevelt refused to intervene to prevent annexation by Japan. Commercial contacts were slight; but Americans predominated in the Protestant missionary forces, and much of the movement for independence was led by Koreans educated under their auspices. American missionaries, and Koreans with whom they had contact, had long been viewed with suspicion by the Japanese.

At the time of Japan's defeat, the Koreans were ill prepared to set up an independent government on which the majority could unite. As with most of the peoples of the Far East, a swelling population made for a basic economic problem and attendant unrest, in spite of the fact that its natural resources provided Korea with a better basis for a satisfactory national economy than China or Japan. The land had been governed by Japan and tied to the economy of that country. Roosevelt, Churchill, and Chiang Kai-shek, at their conference at Cairo in 1943, had declared that their governments were "determined that in due course Korea shall become free and independent." Yet it would be difficult to make that dream a concrete reality.

So far as the American government gave thought to the postwar status of Korea—relatively little while World War II was on—it contemplated a multi-power trusteeship until the country could be put on its feet. It is said on good authority that in the spring of 1945 Russia and the United States agreed to a short trusteeship under themselves, Great Britain, and China. However, in August, 1945, the United States and the Allies had no clear plan for dealing with a liberated Korea. Whatever vague agreement was reached before V-J Day could not be implemented when the surrender of Japan forced immediate decision and action.

Military necessity led to the unhappy division of Korea. On August 10, 1945, only two days after Russia entered the war against Japan, she moved troops into northern Korea. On September 8 American troops landed in the south. It was agreed between the two powers for military purposes that the Russians would operate north of latitude 38° and the Americans south of that line. "The line of demarcation was intended to be temporary," an American Assistant Secretary of State declared, "and only to fix responsibility between the U.S. and the U.S.S.R. for carrying out the Japanese surrender."

In December, 1945, Moscow was the meeting place of a conference between the U.S.S.R., Great Britain, and the United

States. That body authorized a provisional democratic government for Korea under a five-year trusteeship of Great Britain, Russia, the United States, and China. In this agreement China later joined. To implement the plan there was to be a Joint American-Soviet Commission representing the American and Russian commands. The Joint Commission held a number of sessions, but adjourned *sine die* on May 8, 1946. Each command accused the other of being responsible for the failure to agree. Basically the difficulty lay in the desire of each that the projected government should favor its side. In accordance with an earlier agreement, the Americans wished to call in representatives of all Korean parties and social groups for consultation; but the Russians, while desiring the inclusion of pro-Russian elements—a proposal to which the Americans had previously assented—refused to admit Koreans who were critical of the plan for a trusteeship which had been framed at Moscow the previous December. Except for Communist and Communist-dominated groups, all articulate Koreans at first objected to trusteeship and wanted immediate and full independence; therefore, to rule out those opposed to trusteeship would have been to limit the Korean consultants to the pro-Communists and anti-Americans. The Joint Commission again convened in May, 1947. Both the Russians and the Americans had made concessions. However, the disagreement over which Koreans were to be consulted caused the negotiations again to break down.

Now that the Joint Commission had failed, the United States proposed that elections be held in Korea under the United Nations for the formation of a provisional legislature and government. Russia demurred, and countered with the suggestion that the Joint Commission appoint a national assembly from the consultative groups, that by January 1, 1948, both American and Soviet troops be withdrawn, and that the Koreans then conduct their own elections. The United States found this proposal unacceptable and presented the problem to the General Assembly of the United Nations.

In November, 1947, at the instance of the United States and in spite of the urgent objection of the U.S.S.R. and its satellites and their abstention from the voting, the General Assembly of the United Nations took up the issue and voted unanimously to create a United Nations Temporary Commission on Korea. This commission was to hold an election in Korea not later than March 31, 1948, for members of a national assembly, which in turn was to form a national government. The General Assembly put itself on record as favoring an independent Korea and the complete withdrawal of the armed forces of the occupying powers.

In the meantime, two regimes were developing in Korea, separated by the 38th parallel. The Russians acted promptly. Korean sympathizers, including some who had been trained in the U.S.S.R., moved in with their troops and were put in positions of power. Opposition groups were suppressed or, in characteristic fashion, were infiltrated to bring them to support the Communist program. A "people's government" was set up by pro-Russian elements. Strong action was taken against Koreans accused of being pro-Japanese. Industrial reorganization was effected, and land was redistributed to put it into the hands of the cultivators. An army was rapidly developed. The Russians were taking no chances of having a hostile or neutral government in an area on their border and were intent on the North Korean regime taking over the entire country. Tens of thousands of dissidents migrated south of the 38th parallel, thus aggravating the American problem.

The Americans were slower to proceed. They regarded their function as being to disarm and repatriate the Japanese troops and to leave to Korean initiative the setting up of a government. At the outset they recognized no government as being that of

Korea. There were People's Committees which were clearly left-ish, and which were outlawed by the American Military Governor early in the occupation. The Americans used force to suppress the unrest fomented by Communists and pro-Communists, and tended to rely upon conservative politicians, especially Syng-man Rhee, who for years had been abroad agitating for Korean independence. Gradually Koreans were brought into the admini-stration set up by the American military authorities. Elections held in the fall of 1946 returned a conservative majority, ap-parently in part because of pressure by the Korean police. The Americans appointed some members of the Assembly, including moderates and members of the non-Communist left, in an effort to get a more representative body. Maintaining that land reform should be carried out by the Koreans, the Americans did not yield to the demands for the immediate distribution of the large estates among the tenant cultivators. They thus brought down on themselves much criticism. It was not until March, 1948, that the American military government acted to sell to tenant farmers lands which had been owned by the Japanese. This measure affected about one-fourth of the rural population.

The American military government did not entirely mark time. It encouraged the formation of a regime which would gen-uinely represent the majority of the Koreans, and not merely a minority, like the so-called People's Republic in the north. It was faced with an urgent economic situation. Most of the industry was in the north, while the south was primarily agricultural. Yet with a much larger population than the north, soon augmented by refugees from beyond the 38th parallel, it could not even feed itself at the outset. Nor could it produce needed factory products. The American military government was troubled by a rapid rise in prices. Partly to meet the situation, it collected grain from the farmers and rationed it among the consumers. This it did through heavy subsidies. It imported large quantities of food. It sought to revive and stimulate industry. Most of the electric power came from the north. Fortunately this was continued until May, 1948. Then North Korea cut it off. From the beginning of the occupation through July, 1948, the United States provided more than a quarter of a billion dollars in aid for Korea. The Americans also began the rehabilitation and reorganization of the educational system. Curriculums were revised, and textbooks in the native alphabet were provided for the elementary schools to substitute a democratic education for what had been enforced under the Japanese.

The Americans did not wish South Korea to fall into Communist hands, but they did not intend to administer the country permanently. The immediate withdrawal demanded by the Russians would have meant occupation of the South by the North Korean Communists, who were well organized and were determined to take over, when South Korea was not yet in a position to resist them; and it was in an attempt to solve the problem that the Americans had called in the United Nations. The Russians and their supporters loudly denounced this step as a means of perpetuating American control against what they declared to be the will of the Korean people.

Early in 1948 the United Nations Temporary Commission on Korea, which had been set up in pursuance of the action of the General Assembly, reached Korea. It was to have included representatives from Australia, Canada, China, El Salvador, France, India, the Philippines, Syria, and the Ukrainian Soviet Socialist Republic. An Indian was chairman. The Ukrainian delegate refused to serve, saying that no one who could really speak for Korea had been heard, and that the other delegates were "obeying government instructions in most cases favorable to United States policy" and were therefore not neutral. The Commission attempted to visit North Korea and to establish contact with Soviet authorities, for it interpreted the purpose of the United Nations as being one government for all Korea. However, the North Korean and Soviet officials refused to recognize its authority or permit it to go north of the 38th parallel. It therefore determined to hold elections in the part of Korea in which it could operate, namely, the South. The election was held on May 10, 1948. Four-fifths of the South Korean electorate registered, and of these more than nine-tenths voted. The results could be interpreted as expressing the wishes of a large majority of the population. However, before the election there was much violence by Communists and by anti-Communists, and the center and left parties and one rightist party boycotted the election. Hence the numerical returns did not necessarily give so emphatic an indication of the public mind as might at first appear.

The assembly so chosen met and, on July 17, 1948, promulgated a constitution. Under this document a government was set up, with Syngman Rhee as President, which was recognized by the United Nations Commission. To this regime the American military government transferred its responsibilities on August 15; and negotiations were begun for the withdrawal of American troops. The new regime was declared by its constitution to have jurisdiction over all Korea; but, for obvious reasons, it could not extend its administration north of the 38th parallel. The Commission reported to the Assembly of the United Nations, and on December 12, 1948, that body declared by a vote of 48 to 6 that the Republic of Korea (as the new regime was called) was "a lawful government . . . having effective control and jurisdiction over that part of Korea where the Temporary Commission was able to observe and consult and in which the great majority of the people of all Korea reside; that this Government is based on elections which were a valid expression of the free will of the electorate of that part of Korea . . . and that this is the only such Government in Korea." The Assembly also set up a Commission to observe conditions in Korea and to lend its good offices to bring about the unification of the entire country. In doing so, the Assembly came out again for the unification and independence of Korea and the withdrawal of all the occupying forces of foreign powers.

On January 1, 1949, the United States formally recognized the Republic of Korea, and a number of other nations outside the Russian bloc did likewise. The United States gave it extensive aid. Some Americans were employed by it, and the American embassy kept in close touch with it. On December 10, 1948, a few days before formal recognition, the United States signed an agreement with the Republic of Korea for assistance through the Economic Cooperation Administration. Although in 1949 the Congress failed to vote the recommended sum, shipments valued at $126,000,000 were made under the previous army program, and $60,000,000 was advanced through the Reconstruction Finance Corporation. Aid came also through unofficial channels, chiefly through the American churches. In 1950 the Congress authorized $110,000,000 through the Economic Cooperation Administration.

By June, 1950, the Republic of Korea was making substantial gains. Under pressure from the United States to check the mounting inflation, a balanced budget was passed, with increased taxes and reduced expenditures. On the whole, the assistance through the Economic Cooperation Administration was administered wisely. The United Nations Commission reported what it believed to be wholesome signs of the growth of democracy, even though these were in the form of annoying disagreements between the executive and legislative branches of the government. South Korea was producing its own food and was able to ship some grain to Japan.

While this encouraging progress was registered in the South, developments in the North augured ill for the relations between the two sections. On May 1, 1948, on the eve of the elections in the South, the North Korean regime announced a new draft con-

179

stitution for all Korea. Elections to the Supreme People's Democratic Assembly were subsequently carried out in North Korea,
and the North Korean regime claimed that delegates had also
been chosen by a large electorate in the south. In September,
1948, the Supreme People's Democratic Assembly with ostensible
representation from both the North and the South ratified the
draft constitution. Under the new constitution what professed to
be a coalition government was organized with representation
from various parties in what was called the Korean National
Democratic Front. However, there seemed to be no doubt that
the Communists were safely in control, as in similar regimes in
the Soviet bloc. While the structure of the Republic of Korea
showed the influence of the United States, the regime in North
Korea was modeled closely on the Russian pattern.

In October, 1948, the U.S.S.R. gave formal recognition to the
regime in the North; and several of its satellites followed suit.
Russia sought to have it admitted to the United Nations, as vainly
as the friends of the Republic of Korea had sought admission for
that government. At the end of 1948 the U.S.S.R. announced that
it had withdrawn the last of its forces from Korea, leaving a military training mission. North Korea had an army which was said
to be controlled by Russian officers and equipped with Russian
arms. In June, 1949, the United States also withdrew its troops,
but similarly assigned some officers to help train the army of the
Republic of Korea.

Here then, in 1950, were two governments, each claiming to
be the legitimate one for the entire country. That in the South
was recognized by the United Nations and was aided by the
United States. That in the North had the support of Russia and
its satellites. It was clear that friction would be chronic. Some
in the United States were disposed to write off Korea and permit
the Communists to overrun the whole. It was said that the United
States Army had declared South Korea to be indefensible in case

of a war with Russia; and Secretary of State Acheson in an address in January, 1950, seemed to imply that the "defensive perimeter" of the United States from the Aleutians through the Ryukyus and the Philippines did not include either Korea or Formosa. However, he had also said that countries outside this line, if attacked, could rely on the United Nations. Obviously he implied that the United States would support that body. However, the uncertainty of what American action would be and the weakness of the South Korean regime tempted the Communists to act promptly and decisively. Whether they would have done so if they had known that the United States and the United Nations would react vigorously, is debatable.

With dramatic suddenness the issue was forced upon the world on June 25, 1950. The North Korean regime had been agitating for a unified government. The United Nations Commission had offered its services to promote peaceful unification, but had been rebuffed by the North. North Korean troops now marched in force across the 38th parallel. Later the friends of the North Koreans declared that South Korean troops had moved first, and that the North Korean step was defensive. That, however, the majority of the world did not believe.

The North Korean action immediately posed a problem both to the United Nations and to the United States. If North Korea, with the moral and presumably the material support of Russia, were to overrun the South and eliminate a government which had been set up and endorsed by the United Nations, that body would suffer a serious loss of prestige. As in 1931 Japanese action in Manchuria, by demonstrating the weakness of the League of Nations, had dealt that body what in retrospect was seen to have been a deathblow, so now the United Nations, if it proved powerless, would probably crumble; and another attempt to place the relations of nations on the basis of law would be defeated. To many, the long effort of mankind to achieve the lasting peace of which General MacArthur had spoken on that memorable September day a little less than five years before was at stake.

To the United States the issue was fully as momentous. To let the North Koreans carry through with their attack would be to admit defeat in an important round of the struggle to contain Communism. It would be to abandon the people of Korea to Communism and let Russia, through a satellite government, establish itself directly across the Korea Strait from Japan and perhaps prepare for an attack on Japan. The United Nations, to which the United States was committed, would suffer a blow; and the resulting belief through much, perhaps most, of Asia and Europe that the United States tolerated it either from despondent weakness or from isolationism would have facilitated further Communist-Russian advances both in Asia and in western Europe.

On the other hand, defense of South Korea by the United Nations would rest primarily upon the United States. Russia might choose to make it the occasion for starting a general war. American resources, as yet only beginning to be mobilized in an enlarged defense program, might be so engrossed in Korea that Russia could march into western Europe. Korea was far away, and many Americans would be reluctant to engage in a war for a country which seemed to them not to be of vital importance to the United States. Some in the high command of the American armed services believed that the attempt to defend Korea would spread the forces of the United States too thinly and would endanger the defense of what might be more vital spots.

Action by both the United Nations and the United States was immediate and emphatic. At the request of the United States, the Security Council of the United Nations met on the afternoon of June 25. A resolution introduced by the United States was passed by a vote of nine to nothing. Russia had been boycotting the Security Council for its refusal to accept the People's Republic as the representative of China, and Yugoslavia abstained from voting. The resolution called the action of North Korea a "breach of the peace," demanded that that government withdraw its forces to the 38th parallel, and summoned the member governments to give the United Nations "every assistance" in executing the resolution and to abstain from helping North Korea. A few hours later the United States authorized MacArthur to furnish military supplies to South Korea. The United Nations Commission in Korea confirmed the decision of the Security Council by reporting that responsibility for the hostilities clearly rested on North Korea, and asserting that the "South Korean forces were deployed on a wholly defensive basis."

At noon of June 27 President Truman gave out a formal statement declaring that "the attack upon Korea makes it plain beyond all doubt that communism has passed beyond the use of subversion to conquer independent nations and will now use armed invasion and war," that he had "ordered United States air and sea forces to give the Korean Government troops cover and support," and that he had commanded the Seventh Fleet "to prevent any attack on Formosa." He also called on the Chinese Nationalist Government "to cease all air and sea operations against the mainland," saying that "the Seventh Fleet will see that this is done." He declared emphatically that "the determination of the future status of Formosa must await the restoration of security in the Pacific, a peace settlement with Japan, or consideration by the United Nations," and ordered that military aid be speeded up to the Philippines and "France and the associated states in Indo-China."

In sending aid to South Korea, President Truman was clearly in accord with the United Nations; but in his directive concerning Formosa he differed from the policies of some of its important members, notably the United Kingdom. By acting through the United Nations in South Korea the United States greatly enhanced its moral position; but its single-handed procedure in Formosa brought criticism from some of its friends.

The United States appealed to the U.S.S.R. to use its influence to induce the North Koreans to abide by the decision of the United Nations. In a long reply the U.S.S.R. declared that the South Koreans had started the affair by attacking across the 38th parallel, that the United States had planned aggression in Korea, that the vote of the Security Council was illegal, and that before terms of peace were discussed the People's Republic must be given China's seat in the United Nations. In August, Malik, representing the U.S.S.R., returned to the Security Council to assume the chairmanship which came to that country in rotation, attacked the United States vigorously and at length, and insisted that the Chinese People's Republic be admitted to the Council, and that the North Koreans be invited to sit with it to discuss peace terms. The United States declared that the North Koreans must obey the Council and order the withdrawal of their forces before conversations could proceed. To this the U.S.S.R. could not assent, for to have done so would have admitted the legality of the Council's action.

The tide of battle swept back and forth across Korea to the intense suffering of its hapless people. At the outset it looked as though the North Koreans might take the entire country. The South Koreans fought bravely, but were not so heavily equipped. American troops were rushed across the Korea Strait from Japan, but few of them were seasoned warriors. The United States was far away, and time was required, even by air lift, to bring in adequate reenforcements and matériel. Contingents came from several other members of the United Nations, but the major burden fell upon the United States. The air force was clearly superior, but adverse weather hampered its operations. In less than two months the South Koreans and the United Nations had been driven into a small area in the southeast.

By the middle of August, 1950, enough reenforcements had come to enable the United Nations to begin to roll back the North Koreans. They arrived in the nick of time, for the South Koreans now had only a toehold on the mainland. On September 15 the United Nations forces made a sudden and dramatic landing at Inchon, the port of Seoul. Before the end of the month they had taken Seoul. They moved rapidly north, crossed the 38th parallel, and on October 20 took Pyongyang, the North Korean capital. By the end of October their advance forces were approaching the Yalu, the boundary between Manchuria and Korea. For the moment it looked as though all Korea were to be united under the regime sponsored by the United Nations. On October 17, 1950, to calm apprehension in China and elsewhere, especially in Asia, President Truman emphatically said: "Let this be crystal-clear to all—we have no aggressive designs in Korea or in any other place, in the Far East or elsewhere. No country in the world which really wants peace has any reason to fear the United States."

Late in November the tide once more turned. This was because the Chinese Communists stepped in. The presence of some Chinese Communist troops in Korea had been noted as early as October; but it was not until November 26 that the full-scale attack began. Within China the Communists had been intensifying anti-American propaganda. They pictured the United Nations military action in Korea as pure imperialist aggression by the United States. In their minds it was joined with American support to the Nationalists and the blocking by the American fleet of their "liberation" of Formosa. They insisted that the United States had sinister designs on Manchuria. Declaring that American planes had bombed Manchurian centers, they demanded that the United Nations take cognizance of what they alleged were violations of Chinese territory. They appealed for "volunteers" to resist the United States. What both the People's Republic of China and the U.S.S.R. insisted were "volunteers" appeared in large numbers and, supported by Russian-made planes and tanks, pushed back the armies of the United Nations. The Chinese Communists were confident. They had defeated the Nationalists, were "liberating" Tibet, had dealt cavalierly with the property of the United States in Peiping, and had thus far refused to reciprocate the proffered recognition by Great Britain. They demanded that the "American imperialists" be thrown into the sea. They now inflicted the most severe military repulse which Western powers had ever known at the hands of the Chinese. Pyongyang and then Seoul were retaken.

On December 1, 1950, President Truman sent a special message to the Congress in which he denounced Chinese intervention as deliberate and unprovoked aggression. On December 16 he declared that a national emergency existed, requested a meeting of American foreign ministers, and suggested measures for economic warfare against the Chinese Communists.

In other than military ways the United Nations became increasingly involved in the Korean affair and in the issues which arose from it. Although the United States was adamant against admitting the People's Republic to China's seat, it consented to having representatives of the Peiping government come to New York to present to the United Nations its charges against the United States. However, the United States insisted that the People's Republic was an aggressor and demanded that this issue be decided before action was taken on Peiping's case against Washington. No agreement was reached as to which should have priority, and in mid-December, 1950, the Peiping delegation withdrew. That same month the United Nations, against Russian opposition but with American consent, set up a commission at the suggestion of several members to seek a peaceful settlement for Korea. Some governments, including that of India, were fearful that the Korean War would bring on a world-wide conflagration. The commission

was an effort to effect a settlement; it failed, but general war did
not come.

The United States insisted that Communist China be declared
an aggressor, and on February 1, 1951, the United Nations, by a
vote of the General Assembly, complied. The question inevitably
arose as to whether that action should be followed by sanctions.
To impose them entailed the risk of a world war, and there was
great reluctance to undertake them. The United States government believed that at least the exportation of arms to China
should be forbidden, for these would be used against the United
Nations armies in Korea. On May 18, 1951, the United Nations
took the desired action. By a vote of 47 to 0, with eight abstentions
and the Russian bloc not participating, the General Assembly
recommended that every member embargo the shipment to Communist China and North Korea of "arms, ammunition and implements of war, atomic energy materials, petroleum, transportation
materials of strategic value, and items useful in the production of
arms, ammunition and implements of war." However, the decision
was not easily reached. Striking differences appeared, not only
between the Russian bloc and the others, but also between such
major non-Communist powers as the United States, Great Britain,
and India.

The war in Korea went on. United Nations forces, strengthened,
pushed back the enemy. Some of their commanders talked of
"Operation Killer." By this they meant that the casualties of the
enemy, and especially of the Chinese, were far heavier than their
own, and that the Chinese Communists, with an almost inexhaust-
ible reservoir of man power on which to call, were hurling human
fodder against the United Nations guns with disregard to the
cost in lives and must be taught that such tactics could not win
victory.

In the meantime the war in Korea had set off a prolonged
debate in the United States over foreign policy. The issues were

multiform and confused. They centered around the leading role which the United States, because of its wealth and power and its part in World War II and its aftermath, was forced to take in world affairs. The rearming of the United States on which President Truman insisted, the "cold war" between the U.S.S.R. and the United States, now of several years' duration and, far from easing, made more intense by events in Europe and the Far East, could not but provoke discussion. The Communist victory in China was a major defeat for the United States in the struggle with Communism and Russia. Many persons, especially among the Republicans, were disposed to make political capital of it. They vehemently attacked President Truman, declared that the Department of State had adopted a soft policy toward the Chinese Communists, demanded the dismissal of Secretary of State Acheson, and insisted that a vigorous procedure be followed against the Peiping regime. The outbreak of war in Korea, the initial reverses, and the prolongation and indecisive course of the struggle intensified the criticism. Most Americans were bewildered, believed that someone had bungled, and, looking around for a scapegoat, held the Administration responsible.

The debate covered the entire range of American foreign policy, in both Europe and the Far East, but it dealt chiefly with the program of defense, the manner in which the war in the Far East should be waged, especially whether it should be carried into China, and the question whether to deal more drastically with Russia, even at the imminent risk of precipitating another world war.

The debate had really begun before the outbreak of war in Korea. For instance, on January 2, 1950, Senator Knowland of California released a letter from ex-President Hoover saying that the United States must continue to support the National Government of China and should, "if necessary, give it naval protection to the possessions of Formosa, the Pescadores and possibly Hainan Islands." President Truman countered on January 5 by declaring that the United States had no intention of becoming involved in China's civil war by seeking rights or privileges in Formosa, establishing military bases there, or "utilizing its armed forces to interfere in the present situation." Nor would the United States provide "military aid or advice" to the Chinese forces on Formosa, for their resources were already sufficient to obtain "the items which they might consider necessary for the defense of the island." However, Truman added, economic aid would continue.

On April 27, 1950, Hoover, speaking in New York, suggested that either the United Nations should be reorganized without the Communist nations, or else a new united front of anti-Communist countries should be formed in defense of morality, religion, and freedom.

In the winter and spring of 1950–1951 the debate broke out in full vigor. On December 12, 1950, Joseph P. Kennedy, former American Ambassador to Great Britain, said that current American policy was bankrupt, that the United Nations was a failure, that the supposed friends of the United States were ungrateful, and that the United States should withdraw from its "unwise commitments" in Korea, Berlin, and the defense of western Europe. On December 20, 1950, four days after President Truman had declared the existence of a national emergency and the day after General Eisenhower had been appointed Supreme Commander of the Allied forces in Europe, ex-President Hoover startled the world with a speech in which he demanded that not another man or another dollar be sent to the nations of western Europe until they themselves had organized armies strong enough to provide a "sure dam against the red flood," and that, instead, the United States should retire to the defense of the western hemisphere by holding the Atlantic and Pacific oceans. This was to be accomplished by an outer rim of defenses which would embrace Japan, Formosa, and the Philippines on the Pacific side, and Britain on the Atlantic side. The other members of the British Commonwealth were also to be included in the program for defense. To implement the defense, there was to be rearmament in the sea and air.

Many in the United States hailed Hoover's pronouncement with enthusiasm. It was also acclaimed in the U.S.S.R. However, President Truman and Secretary of State Acheson sharply dissented. The former described it as isolationism, and the latter characterized it obliquely as being tantamount to "sitting quivering in a storm cellar waiting for whatever fate others may wish to prepare for us."

The great debate came to a climax over MacArthur. As the general most closely associated in the American mind with the loss and recovery of the Philippines, as the commander, embodiment, and director, almost dictator, of the occupation of Japan, and as the commander of the United Nations forces in Korea, MacArthur held a unique position. For some time it had been clear that he disagreed with the policies of the Truman Administration in Korea and China. He embarrassed the Administration by public utterances which ran counter to its mind. At the end of July, 1950, MacArthur visited Chiang Kai-shek on Formosa. This display of cordiality aroused a flutter of excitement. It sent Assistant Secretary of State W. Averell Harriman on a special flight to Tokyo and called forth official denials that the affair had political significance. Late in August, 1950, MacArthur issued a lengthy public statement to the national encampment of the Veterans of Foreign Wars saying that, as he saw it, to permit Formosa to fall into the hands of a "hostile foreign power" would be catastrophic. In October, 1950, President Truman journeyed to the Pacific and met with General MacArthur on Wake Island to come to a meeting of minds.

Many later blamed MacArthur for crossing the 38th parallel

and pushing close to the Chinese border in disregard of known Chinese Communist sensibilities, and for not taking account of the assembling of the Chinese forces in Manchuria which in November brought the disheartening retreat to the armies of the United Nations. MacArthur was clearly restive over instructions from Washington not to bomb Chinese installations in what he called the "privileged sanctuary" of Manchuria.

As time passed it became increasingly obvious that the Administration and MacArthur were not in accord. MacArthur believed that the entrance of Communist China into Korea had really begun a new war, a war of Communist China against the United States. He was convinced that the war could not be won by confining it to Korea. He would bomb whatever centers in China would weaken that country, blockade China's ports, and encourage Chiang Kai-shek's forces to invade the mainland. MacArthur believed that the defeat of Communism in China would save Europe.

However, the procedure which MacArthur proposed would entail a risk of war with Russia, especially in view of the treaty between the U.S.S.R. and the People's Republic of February, 1950, by which the signatories pledged themselves that, in the event of aggression on either of the two by Japan or another power allied with Japan, the other would immediately render military or other aid with all means at its disposal. While that pact would not certainly bind Russia to go to war in the event of the adoption of the measures advocated by MacArthur, and the U.S.S.R. would experience no difficulty in finding another pretext if it wished war, such action might be used as a convenient excuse. Moreover, such a procedure against the Chinese Communist regime might so engross American resources that the aid of the United States to western Europe would be sufficiently curtailed to tempt Russia to move into that area, already insecure. MacArthur had said, like some of those who supported him, that he was opposed to putting American ground forces in China; but, once large-scale operations were begun, such forces would almost certainly be sent to push advantages won by sea and air. The United States would probably thus become bogged down in China much as Japan had been. In addition, intense suffering would be inflicted upon millions of Chinese who were not Communists. Even if Russia kept out of the war, the cost to the United States in treasure and lives would be prodigious, and additional ill will in China toward America would be created. These were among the considerations which led the Administration to differ from MacArthur.

MacArthur further embarrassed President Truman. On December 6, 1950, the Joint Chiefs of Staff, in pursuance of an order from the President, directed that a broad list of officials in the field as well as in Washington should release no speech, press release, or other public statement concerning foreign policy until it received clearance from the Department of State, and no speech, press release, or other public statement on military matters until it was cleared by the Department of Defense, and that they should send advance copies also to the White House. The President also directed that "officials overseas, including military commanders, . . . should be ordered to exercise extreme caution in public statements, to clear all but routine statements with their departments, and to refrain from direct communication on military or foreign policy with newspapers, magazines, or other publicity media in the United States."

However, late in March, 1951, while Washington was in delicate conversations with thirteen other members of the United Nations who had troops in Korea concerning negotiations which might lead to peace in that country, General MacArthur offered, quite independently, to meet the Commander in Chief of the enemy forces "in an earnest effort to find any military means whereby the realization of the political objectives of the United

Nations in Korea, to which no nation may justly take exceptions, might be accomplished without further bloodshed." MacArthur's statement made necessary the abandonment of the Administration's plan.

A few days later, on April 5, Congressman Martin of Massachusetts placed in the *Congressional Record* a letter dated March 20, 1951, in which MacArthur expressed accord with him on the utilization of the Chinese forces on Formosa.

The accumulation of incidents of this kind in which a general in the field disregarded the wishes and commands of the President, by constitutional provision the Commander in Chief of the army and navy, could not well be ignored. Such a conflict, repeatedly made public, between the President and MacArthur weakened the United States in the Far East and Europe and in its home constituency. To allow MacArthur to control would be to adopt a policy in the Far East which was almost certainly less desirable than that of the President. Even more, it would be a surrender of the President to a general, would weaken the civilian elements in the government as against the military, and—by its disregard of the Constitution—would jeopardize the very democracy for which the United States and the United Nations were fighting. On April 11, 1951, therefore, the President recalled General MacArthur and appointed General Matthew B. Ridgway in his place.

That step brought an immediate outcry. MacArthur was already a national hero. For the moment he became even more so. President Truman knew that this would be the initial reaction, and counted on the calm judgment of the majority eventually to rally to him. Many Republicans were vocal in their denunciation, and a few advocated impeachment proceedings against the President. MacArthur accepted the Presidential mandate, returned to the United States, and made his defense before the Congress in a masterly address which was broadcast to the nation.

The great debate over foreign policy came to a crescendo, with many speeches and statements. In addition, the Armed Services and Foreign Relations committees of the Senate held joint hearings during May and June at which most of the principals in the Far Eastern policies of the past six years or more were asked to make statements and were submitted to interrogation. Outstanding was the testimony of MacArthur and of George C. Marshall, Secretary of Defense. Most of what was said was made public. It spoke volumes for the soundness of American democracy that the debate and the hearings could be carried through without tumult. In a totalitarian government MacArthur would have been "liquidated," and a united front presented to the world. In the Senate hearings, in contrast, wide diversities of view were frankly brought out.

The issues were in part clarified. It was obvious that Marshall sided with Truman, and that the recall of MacArthur had been made only after consultations and with full agreement with him and those closest to him. The Chairman of the Joint Chiefs of Staff, General Omar N. Bradley, for example, declared that to have followed MacArthur's plans would have involved the United States with Communist China "in the wrong war, at the wrong place, at the wrong time, and with the wrong enemy."

In the main the Truman Administration continued the policy which it had earlier pursued. However, it gradually made some concessions. It did not cease giving priority to western Europe. Nor did it bomb Chinese cities, blockade Chinese ports, or utilize the Chinese Nationalist armies on the mainland. Yet it stepped up its aid to the Nationalists on Formosa, not only in the economic realm but also by sending a military mission and increasing the flow of arms.

On the eve of the anniversary of the outbreak of the Korean War a hint came through Russia that the Communists might be willing to consider an armistice. Negotiations were begun, and representatives for the belligerents met at Kaesong, a spot suggested by the Communists, south of the 38th parallel. Many hitches occurred in the negotiations. The Communists demanded that as a prelude to an armistice both sides agree to a withdrawal of all foreign troops from Korea. The United Nations commander declared that this was a political, not a military, issue, and that he would not discuss it. There was also marked dissent over the boundary along which a demilitarized zone should be created. The Communists stood for the 38th parallel. The United Nations commander insisted that it be north of that line, more nearly where the forces of the United Nations were then deployed, saying that from the military standpoint it was more defensible. Negotiations continued, with interruptions, through 1951; but by the end of the year only partial agreement had been reached, and crucial issues were still to be resolved.

The Korean War was the most severe test which the United Nations had thus far met. In it that body displayed the ability to bring together the forces of a large number of nations, under a unified command, and in support of a world organization to resist aggression. Here was a significant step, even though only a step, toward the achievement of world order and the rule of law in relations among nations.

Selected Bibliography

Department of State, *Korea, 1945–1948: A Report on Political Developments and Economic Resources with Selected Documents* (Washington, 1948).

Department of State, *United States Policy in the Korean Crisis* (Washington, 1950).

Department of State, *United States Policy in the Korean Conflict, July 1950 to February 1951* (Washington, 1951).

G. M. McCune and A. L. Grey, *Korea Today* (Cambridge: Harvard University Press, 1950).

Military Situation in the Far East: Hearings before the Committee on *Armed Services and the Committee on Foreign Relations, United States Senate, Eighty-second Congress, First Session, to Conduct an Inquiry into the Military Situation in the Far East and the Facts Surrounding the Relief of General of the Army Douglas MacArthur from His Assignments in that Area.* (Washington, 5 parts, 1951).

L. K. Rosinger and associates, *The State of Asia: A Contemporary Survey* (New York: Alfred A. Knopf, 1951).

R. H. Rovere and A. M. Schlesinger, Jr., *The General and the President* (New York: Farrar, Straus & Young, 1951).

R. P. Stebbins and the Research Staff of the Council on Foreign Relations, *The United States in World Affairs, 1950* (New York: Harper & Brothers, 1951).

XI. A TENTATIVE APPRAISAL

IN THE SIX MOMENTOUS YEARS AFTER THE DEFEAT
of Japan, to what extent was the United States frustrated, and
how far was it successful in the Far East? To what degree did
American policy fail, and where had it achievement to its credit?

It must be clear that one of the historic dreams of Americans
had not been realized. The markets of that region and especially
those of China, the potentialities of which had so long lured
Americans eastward, had not proved to be profitable. If results
were measured in terms of the dimensions of trade and investments, the verdict would have to be stark and tragic failure.
Returns in dollars and cents were only a minute fraction of the
financial cost of the operations in the Pacific and the Far East
during World War II and afterward. Even had they been hundreds of times larger, they would have been poor recompense for
the expenditure of lives. Nor was there any prospect that in the
foreseeable future the returns would attain much larger dimensions. Americans had depended on the Far East for important
raw materials, notably rubber, tin, and quinine, but World War
II proved that in a pinch substitutes or other sources could be
found.

What of the other and more basic concerns which had been
much more prominent in the Far Eastern policy of the United
States, especially since V-J Day—the welfare of the peoples of
these regions and the containment of Communism? Here the
record was uneven. It contained both defeats and victories. For
neither was the ledger closed. Some of the defeats might prove
to be only temporary, although spectacular, reverses, and from
the perspective of a later day what appeared in 1951 to be achievements might be illusory.

The American Record in the Far East, 1945–1951

In China, the largest single unit of population in the world, long the major concern in the Far East of Americans and of their government, a palpable defeat had been suffered. In India, Pakistan, Burma, Thailand, Malaya, Indochina, and Indonesia, where the United States had only recently begun to play an active role, the record was uneven and inconclusive. Thus far, on the whole, the balance seemed favorable. In the Philippines, the verdict was of necessity tentative. The achievements had been real and important, but their stability was by no means assured. To date the postwar record in Japan was one of striking success; but the obstacles were formidable, part of the success was qualified by weaknesses and compromises, and it would have been rash to assert that the gains would be permanent. The year 1951 was too early for more than a very preliminary appraisal of Korea. The Korean people had been sufferers, partly as an aftermath of Japanese rule, partly from Communism, partly from American blundering, and partly from their own ineptitude. Yet in South Korea distinct gains were being made when the storm from the north broke upon it.

To all thoughtful and informed observers at least three features of the record must be clear. The first was the limited and doubtful value of armed force unless it was accompanied by wide political, cultural, and economic policies and made the instrument for the support and protection of those policies. Even with this qualification the utility of its results was highly questionable. American armed action in the Far East had produced great changes; but it was at least arguable that in the last analysis it had neither served the interests of the peoples of those areas nor curbed Communism.

The defeat of Japan undoubtedly freed the peoples of the Far East, including the Japanese themselves, from the tyranny of aggressive Japanese militarism. In southeast Asia the Japanese occupation and propaganda broke up the patterns of European colonial imperialism, and the defeat of the Japanese gave opportunity for the early achievement of independence and self-government. However, colonial rule was on the way out and, as in India and Pakistan, almost certainly would have disappeared had there never been a Japanese occupation and defeat. A slower transition might have been better for the peoples of these areas and have been followed by more stable and democratic regimes than those which emerged from World War II.

In China American entrance into the struggle against Japan made possible the triumph of Communism. Had the Japanese been permitted to continue their effort to raise up a puppet regime which would cooperate with them, no one can say what the result for China would have been. That Japan could not permanently have imposed her will on China seems clear. How long it would have taken the Chinese to throw off the Japanese yoke, and what manner of China would have emerged, must be conjectural. It may be that even then Communism would have been the victor. As it was, American participation in the war to expel the Japanese was followed by the capture of China by Communism and thereby worked against both the welfare of the Chinese and the containment of Communism. Nor, as we have said, when once the defeat of Japan had been made sure, could any program adopted by the United States short of a complete and costly occupation of China have prevented the Communists from taking the country. The application of armed force might prevent the further spread of Communism, as it did at least for a time in Korea and Indochina; but at best it would aggravate rather than solve the basic ills on which Communism fed and could only give opportunity for the forces which could heal them to work.

A second feature of the record can be summarized in the words of General MacArthur on that historic September 2, 1945. General MacArthur declared, "The problem basically is theological."

Coming from an eminent military man and not from a clergyman or a professional theologian, the words took on peculiar significance. In their broadest sense they were undoubtedly true. The outcome in the Far East as in the rest of the world would be determined primarily not by armies, navies, or air power, but by what men really believed concerning the universe, the nature of man, and the relation of men to one another and to the universe. It was convictions concerning these fundamental issues that shaped and gave drive to Communism. American and British democracy were largely the products of one kind of Christianity— what is sometimes termed Puritanical Protestantism or, not with strict accuracy, Calvinism. The ideals of that form of Protestantism were chiefly responsible for the revolution of the seventeenth century which gave shape and impetus to English democracy and formed the ideals which underlay the American Revolution and the American dream. Similarly, each of the peoples of the Far East had inherited convictions, some Buddhist, some Hindu, some Confucian, some Taoist, some Moslem, others from one or another form of animism. These were shaken by the forces from the West, but to a lesser or greater extent they survived. In varying degrees they would enter into the new forms of the changing cultures of the Far East.

All this meant that American democracy could not be completely reproduced in the Far East, and that at best the basic principles which to Americans were axiomatic—such as the worth of the individual, the combination of liberty and responsibility, freedom of speech and assembly, and the formation of public opinion through uninhibited discussion—could be realized only slowly. Those citizens of Far Eastern countries who through missionaries or education in the United States had imbibed the fundamental convictions which underlay American democracy constituted a small minority. They had an effect, often much more substantial than their numbers would seem to warrant; but even in them what had been adopted from abroad was mingled with what had been inherited. The result was a compound of both the old and the new.

If American democracy could not be fully reproduced in any land in the Far East, and if what was introduced would eventually be modified, so Communism, heady wine though it was, would eventually be in part denatured and diluted. In China and other Far Eastern lands where it became dominant, it would eventually be one element in a fresh combination of the ancient heritage with what had entered from the West. The revolutions which were so prominent in the Far East, and which were producing such startling and kaleidoscopic changes, would not sweep away all that had gone before. Americans could hope, and not without cause, that much of what they believed to be true about man and the universe would have profound effects west of the Pacific; but they would do well not to be misled by superficial alterations, spectacular though these might be, either to complacent optimism or to defeatist despair.

A third feature of the record was the importance of the economic factor. One did not need to be a Communist or to assert the supremacy of economics in shaping the destiny of mankind in order to recognize the importance of livelihood in influencing the course of events in the Far East, both present and future. The pressure of growing populations on subsistence, the demands of millions for more of the material means to make existence at least tolerable and if possible enjoyable, would have to be reckoned with as causes of domestic unrest and revolution and of complications in the international scene. The very fact that the economic problems could not be easily or quickly solved rendered them the more insistent.

A fourth feature of the record was the mistakes and ambiguities in the policies and procedures of the United States. These arose partly from the fact that Americans, being human, were far from

perfect, and partly from the weaknesses of the democratic processes as Americans understood and practiced them. Years ago it
was said that the differences between a totalitarian government
and a democratic regime as found in the United States are those
between a great steamer built without watertight compart-
ments and a raft of logs. The first seems to be more efficient but
may founder if it strikes a single mine or rock. In contrast those
afloat on the raft always have their feet wet and make slow progress; but they can be reasonably sure that their craft will not
break up or sink.

Among the weaknesses of the United States were occasional
failures to consult the governments with which it was associated,
and at times unwillingness to take account of the effect of American decisions upon friendly powers who had to bear the conse-
quences. Another was the frequent lack of clarity and consistency
in policy. This was puzzling to friends, neutrals, and enemies and
dangerous to a high degree. Much of it arose from many conflicting currents and opinions in the United States, the multiplicity
of branches of the government which had a voice in shaping
policies and decisions, the pressure groups, and the contest for
power between the two major parties. Two of the many instances
were the apparent "military abandonment of Korea" before the
invasion from the north began and the confusion over whether
the United Nations forces, led by an American commander,
should stop when in their counteradvance they reached the 38th
parallel.

Some of the confusion was due to imperfections in carrying
through the bipartisan policy, especially after Senator Vanden-
berg's illness and death. Some of it was ascribable to inadequate
preparation and consequent fumbling in the public statements
of responsible officials. As we have more than once pointed out,
the record was not entirely one of fumbling, indecisiveness, and
failure, but it had in it much of all three. The statement ascribed

to a distinguished European statesman of the seventeenth century, "With how little wisdom is the world governed!" could be applied to the United States as to other countries, and in its procedures in the Far East as elsewhere.

In view of these and other features of the situation, it was clear that Americans should not expect early release from the Far East. They tended to be dogmatic and to demand quick returns. That might be a result of being citizens of a new country. Here cities rose almost overnight. Within a generation, new commonwealths were settled and were admitted as states. By long habit Americans impatiently demanded that they get on with a job, complete it, and turn to another enthralling opportunity. For better or worse, they were in the Far East and could not get out. They were there in lands of ancient cultures and of gigantic revolutions to which no early termination was possible. Of these revolutions Americans of the current generation could hope to see only stages, not the end.

As we noted at the outset, the problems were such as to admit of no early, easy, or completely satisfactory solutions. The appalling increases in population would not quickly stop—unless by inconceivably tragic slaughter, pestilence, and famine. Poverty at best could only gradually be alleviated through industrialization and better handling of the soil. The needed education would not be rapidly acquired. Experience in self-government would be painful in former colonial areas. In one form or another, Communism was probably to be in Asia for many years. What Americans did through private channels or through their government could have immense influence but could be only one group of factors in determining the outcome. Millions of Americans would need to make themselves familiar with the main outlines of these problems, for only thus could their form of democracy operate intelligently. They would have to be patient and not expect perfection of their representatives or a quick release from their perplexities and burdens. They would need to be prepared to adjust their policies to changing circumstances. Yet there was no cause to despair of a main sense of direction and of accomplishments which would be worthy of the hour with which they had been matched.

Index

Index

Index